# THE MIDDLER

# THE MIDDLER

## KIRSTY APPLEBAUM

HENRY HOLT AND COMPANY
New York

Henry Holt and Company, *Publishers since 1866*

Henry Holt® is a registered trademark of Macmillan Publishing Group, LLC

120 Broadway, New York, NY 10271 • mackids.com

Library of Congress Cataloging-in-Publication Data

Names: Applebaum, Kirsty, author.
Title: The middler / Kirsty Applebaum.
Description: First American edition. | New York : Henry Holt and Company, 2020. | "Published in Great Britain by Nosy Crow in 2019." | Summary: Eleven-year-old Maggie, a middle-born child where only the eldest are valued, has her world turned upside-down by forbidden friendship with Una, a wanderer girl from outside the boundaries of Fennis Wick.
Identifiers: LCCN 2019019334| ISBN 978-1-250-31733-9 (hardcover) | ISBN 978-1-250-24816-9 (audio book) | ISBN 978-1-250-24815-2 (audio download)
Subjects: | CYAC: Middle-born children—Fiction. | Brothers and sisters—Fiction. | Friendship—Fiction. | Fantasy.
Classification: LCC PZ7.1.A653 Mid 2020 | DDC [Fic]—dc23
LC record available at https://lccn.loc.gov/2019019334

Our books may be purchased in bulk for promotional, educational, or business use. Please contact your local bookseller or the Macmillan Corporate and Premium Sales Department at (800) 221-7945 ext. 5442 or by email at MacmillanSpecialMarkets@macmillan.com.

First edition, 2020 / Designed by Katie Klimowicz

Printed in the United States of America by LSC Communications, Harrisonburg, Virginia

10  9  8  7  6  5  4  3  2  1

*For Jacqui C.*

# Prologue

Our eldest, Jed, got born first out of all of us.

Our youngest, Trig—he got born four years later.

And me, Maggie, I was in between. The middler, worst luck.

# Monday,
# September 1

# Chapter 1

I took my summer diary out of my drawer. Nearly all the sheets of paper matched. On the very last page I'd drawn a picture of a red admiral. It had black wings and bright red stripes, just like the ones we'd seen up at the butterfly fields.

I straightened the yellow wool bow that held it all together and ran my hands over the front to flatten it down. I wouldn't win Best Diary—an eldest always wins that—but maybe I could get runner-up. I carried it downstairs.

"You ready, Mags?" Trig had the front door open and was leaning right out of it, both hands gripping the doorframe. His diary was on the doormat, tied up with garden string. "We should've left already. Shouldn't we, Dad? We should've left."

"Oh, Maggie." Dad shook his head at my legs. "We really need to do something about that uniform. It's even shorter than it was before the holidays."

He yanked at the bottom of my dress. It shrugged back up again.

"Jed! Jed! Jed!" Trig was turning red with all his shouting.

"Just a minute!" Jed's voice echoed down the stairs.

Mom came out of the kitchen, booted up for a day in the fields. "Leave without him," she said. "It's his own fault if he's late."

"C'mon, Maggie." Trig picked up his diary, but I wasn't going anywhere till Jed was with us.

Eventually he appeared, shirt hanging out and jam on his chin.

"Did you remember your summer diary?" said Trig.

"S'in here." Jed turned round and patted his back pocket. His messy, folded pages flapped out of the top.

Dad went to wipe the jam off Jed's face, but Jed ducked under his arm and we all ran through the door into the warm September air.

Trig was hopeless at running. He held his diary right out in front of him all the way to school. Me and Jed had to stop at every corner for him to catch up.

~ ~ ~

*"Good morning, Mrs. Zimmerman;*
*Good morning, Mr. Temple;*
*Good morning, Miss Conteh;*
*Good morning, Mr. Webster;*
*Good morning, EVERYONE."*

The school hall smelled like the beginning of term. Wood oil and scouring powder.

"Smells weird. Doesn't it, Maggie? Doesn't it, Jed? Smells weird." Trig fidgeted and scrunched up his nose.

"Shhh," I said.

Lindi Chowdhry was in front of us, all cross-legged and

straight-backed and long-haired. Her dress had a new frill sewn round the hem. Jed scooted forward so he was sitting closer to her.

Mrs. Zimmerman clasped her hands together in front of her waist. "Mr. Webster has kindly spent part of his summer sanding and oiling our hall floor. Aren't we lucky?"

I spread out my fingers and pressed my palms onto the smooth wood. *Must've taken him ages.*

"Heads down, please, for the morning chant."

> *"Our eldests are heroes.*
> *Our eldests are special.*
> *Our eldests are brave.*
>
> *Shame upon any who holds back an eldest,*
> *And shame upon their kin.*
> *Most of all,*
> *Shame upon the wanderers.*
>
> *Let peace settle over the Quiet War,*
> *Truly and forever."*

Mrs. Zimmerman lifted her head, tilted it to one side, and smiled. "Welcome back to Fennis Wick School, everyone. I hope you enjoyed your break."

We bit at our nails and gazed up at the empty walls while she said all the things that principals have to say at the beginning of term.

"Mr. Webster has also dug over the toilets for us. Please be sure to use the new ones and leave the old ones to compost."

We clapped for Mr. Webster.

"Miss Conteh has returned to us after having her baby—a little boy, named Michael. An eldest. We're hoping his dad might pop in with him one lunchtime."

We clapped for Miss Conteh.

"Two of our pupils, Sally Owens and Deb Merino—both eldests, of course—turned fourteen over the summer and have gone to camp."

We clapped for Sally Owens.

We clapped for Deb Merino.

"And two more of our eldests are heading off to camp this very Saturday—Jed Cruise and Lindi Chowdhry."

Jed leaned in and nudged shoulders with Lindi.

My hands were getting fed up with all the clapping.

"And just before we return to our classes, we have a special guest here today with some important news." Mrs. Zimmerman held out an arm toward the entrance of the hall.

No one came out.

"Er . . . *We have a special guest here with some important news*," she said again, louder this time.

No one came out.

Mr. Temple cleared his throat. He nodded toward the window.

Mayor Anderson was sitting on the wall in the littlests' outdoor play area, feet resting on a go-fast-kart and two hands cupped round an enormous sandwich. Cheese, by the look of it. She finished up chewing, swallowed her mouthful, and gave us a wave.

A few of us waved back.

Mrs. Zimmerman took a deep breath in. "Would you be so kind as to let the mayor know we're ready for her, Mr. Temple?"

~ ~ ~

"Okay." Mayor Anderson stood in the middle of Mr. Webster's newly oiled floor, her hair drawn back in a straggly ponytail. "I'm not going to beat around the bush and do all that *What have you learned over the summer?* rubbish. I'll leave that to your teachers, eh?" She gave us a wink and got a few sniggers back from the audience.

Mrs. Zimmerman closed her eyes.

"But what I am going to do," the mayor went on, "is tell you we've heard reports of wanderers five miles south of the town boundary."

*Wanderers?*

The sniggering stopped.

Mrs. Zimmerman opened her eyes.

A shiver crept across my shoulders.

"Yep." Mayor Anderson nodded. "Yesterday I was up at the city. Met with some colleagues. It's been a while since we had wanderers in our area but their numbers appear to be increasing." She took a slow moment to look from one side of the hall to the other, catching as many of our eyes as she could.

"So," she carried on, "why do we not want wanderers nearby? Anyone?"

Trig stuck his arm up as high as he could get it. Pushed it even higher with his other hand. Mayor Anderson couldn't miss him.

"Go on, then—tell us, Trig."

"They're . . . er"—Trig looked up to the ceiling, the way you do when you're trying hard to remember something—"*dirty*, *dangerous*, and . . . *deceitful*."

"Dirty. Dangerous. Deceitful." Mayor Anderson boomed the words back at us, counting them off on her fingers as she went. "At camp, our eldests join the Quiet War. They fight valiantly. They fight heroically. They fight so that we, back home, can remain safe. My one and only child, Caroline, went to camp ten years ago this very month. I couldn't be more proud."

We clapped for Caroline.

The mayor held up a hand.

"Wanderers," she said, "are protected from the enemy by our brave heroes—but they selfishly keep their own eldests close." She lowered her hand to her hip. "They disobey Andrew Solsbury's edict that decrees we must ALL send our eldests to camp. They deny their families the opportunity to live in a town in a civilized manner, and they deny their eldests the opportunity to fight for their country. They are dirty, dangerous, and deceitful. Do we want their kind anywhere near us, here in Fennis Wick?"

"No, Mayor Anderson." We shook our heads.

"And more than that"—the mayor leaned in toward us and lowered her voice to a whisper—"much more than that—you're aware of the horror wreaked by wanderers the last time they ventured close to Fennis Wick. My own sister was among the casualties." She dropped her eyes to the floor.

A littlest at the front began to cry.

Trig's knees started jiggling.

"So." The mayor took a deep breath and lifted her head. "What can we do to keep ourselves safe? What's the most important rule of all?"

"Never go beyond the boundary!" Trig burst out the answer.

"Abso-bloomin-lutely, Trig Cruise. *Never go beyond the boundary*. Follow that rule and you'll be safe from wanderers. Remember: dirty, dangerous, deceitful. All right?"

"Yes, Mayor Anderson," we nodded.

She smiled. One of those smiles where the sides of your mouth go down instead of up.

"So, how about we sing the boundary song to finish?" Mayor Anderson rubbed her hands together. "Mr. Temple? Would you accompany us on the old piano? Still working, is it?"

Mr. Temple lifted the lid of the piano. He interlaced his fingers and turned them inside out. The clicking echoed all around the hall.

"Oh—a quick reminder before we start singing." Mayor Anderson wasn't smiling anymore. She ran her tongue across the front of her teeth. "Going beyond a town boundary isn't only a risk to yourself—it puts the whole of Fennis Wick in danger. Your friends, your family, your neighbors. And anyone who puts Fennis Wick in danger could be subject to a very serious punishment indeed. So let's keep everyone safe, eh? Now, carry on, Mr. Temple."

The crying littlest cried even louder.

~ ~ ~

Back in the classroom, Miss Conteh talked about the time before the Quiet War and what summer holidays were like then. She said people used to go to other countries on airplanes. I doodled a picture of an airplane in the bottom corner of my slate. Licked my finger and rubbed it off.

Sometimes I wondered if teachers just made stuff up.

After break Miss Conteh asked for our summer diaries. She walked between the desks, collecting them and piling them up in her arms.

"I'll be reading through these this afternoon," she said, "and tomorrow I'll announce the winners."

I passed her mine, taking care to keep the bow straight.

"Thank you, Maddie."

*Maddie?*

Lindi laughed. "It's *Maggie*, Miss Conteh, not Maddie."

"Oh, of course it is. Sorry, Maggie, the baby had me up four times last night."

She put my diary on the pile, then stuck six more right on top of it, squashing the bow.

# Chapter 2

After school we changed out of our uniforms and went up to the cemetery, right out near the hawthorn boundary. Hunting for wanderers.

It was Jed's idea.

"Come on," he called down. "Who's coming up next?"

He was balanced in the tallest tree, legs dappled by the leaves and the sun. Looked like he was wearing camouflage. The branches rippled in the heat.

Me and Trig and Lindi all squinted up.

"Look." Jed pointed south, past the red-berried hawthorn. Grandad Cruise's watch glinted on his wrist. "I can see for miles."

My heart *kerdunk-kerdunk-kerdunk*ed under my T-shirt.

"Can you see any wanderers?" Trig shaded his eyes with both hands.

"Course not, not yet," said Jed. "We've got to watch and wait."

He was up really high. My stomach swirled just looking at him.

"D'you think the mayor'll give us a reward?" I shaded my

eyes too. "Y'know, if we find one? Will she read our names out in assembly?"

Jed laughed. "You're never going to spot one, Maggie. You're just a middler. You're too scared to even climb up here."

"Yeah, you're always too scared of everything." Lindi elbowed me and Trig out of the way. "Watch out, Jed. I'm coming up next."

Jed grinned. It was his idea of heaven, sitting on a branch with Lindi all to himself.

She walked between the two graves set under the tree. The headstones had ancient names carved into them: WILLIAM WHIT-TINGTON and GEORGINA MILLICENT CRUISE. Georgina Millicent Cruise was my great-great-great-great-grandmother. Funny how the cemetery smelled of grass and soil and sap-laden trees, when actually we were surrounded by old, dead relatives.

Lindi got a knotty handhold on the trunk and found somewhere to put her first foot. She pulled herself up and found a second foothold, then a third, a fourth, a fifth. She didn't have shorts on like me. She was wearing a stupid white dress that showed her underwear if she even just climbed over a fence.

She was nearly up to Jed. My mouth went dry.

They were right—I was scared. Of climbing. Of hunting for wanderers. Of everything. So what, though? So what? We were never going to find one anyway.

Jed held out his hand to Lindi. She grabbed it. She leaned away from the trunk and let go with her other hand.

Her foot slipped on the dry bark.

Their hands slid apart.

Her stupid dress blew up around her waist.

She bounced headfirst off the William Whittington gravestone and landed on the ground, blood all over her face.

She lay there, still as you like.

The sound her head had made on the gravestone replayed itself in my ears. *Crunck.* Like being whacked with a brick. *Crunck.*

Her underwear was white, with little blue flowers on it. Forget-me-nots. I stepped forward and pulled her dress down. It wasn't right for the boys to be seeing all that.

~ ~ ~

No one screamed. No one shouted. Jed said something unrepeatable, but he said it really quiet, like his voice had been squashed by the shock. Then he half scrambled, half jumped down from the tree. He tried pulling Lindi up but he couldn't lift her. Her blood got all over his hands. He pushed his hair out of his eyes and left a messy red stripe across the side of his head.

"Lindi," he said in his squashed voice. "Lindi. Lindi. Lindi."

"She's dead," I said.

"No she's not; she can't be," said Jed. "We have to do something."

And we stood there, all three of us Cruise kids, looking down at Lindi Chowdhry with her white dress and her bloody face and her long, dark hair spread out on the grass.

"You have to check if she's breathing." It was Trig—Trig, who can't even hop or run or tie proper reef knots. "If she's not, you have to breathe for her. First aid. We did it in school, remember? Ages ago." He swallowed. "And one of us has to run for help."

Jed knelt down next to Lindi. "I'm not leaving her. You go, Maggie."

*Me?*

"Quick, Maggie—you gotta run."

So I ran.

~ ~ ~

I ran through the cemetery, leaping over the old Parker graves and the Stanbury ones too, grass whipping at my ankles. I ran all down the edge of Anderson's field. Tiny black thunderbugs flew into my eyes but I didn't stop to scrape them out, I just blinked and kept running. At the bottom of the field I jumped over the sun-dried mud ridges and didn't trip even once. I skimmed round the side of the old caravan park south of the town, all the time shouting.

"Help! Help! Dr. Sunita!"

I gasped gobfuls of hot, woolly air. I shouted for Mrs. Chowdhry too.

"Mrs. Chowdhry! Mrs. Chowdhry!"

I leaped across the vegetable plots, between zucchini, rhubarb, tomatoes.

"What is it, girl?"

I stopped so quick I nearly fell over.

It was Elsie Weather, kneeling in the strawberry beds. Just my luck.

"What is it, girl? What's wrong?" She used her stick to help herself up. She had two old sponges strapped to her knees with rubber bands.

"It's Lindi, Lindi Chowdhry. I need to get help."

"Wait, girl. Perhaps old Elsie can be of use." She brushed some earth off her knee sponges.

"I have to be quick. Lindi hit her head. She fell out of a tree. She's not moving." I clattered out sentences in the wrong order, glancing over toward the town.

Elsie Weather swapped her stick from one unsteady hand to the other, reached into her pocket, and brought out a hanky. She coughed into it, like she was coughing up her insides. My legs quivered, ready to run.

"Lindi Chowdhry." She refolded her hanky. Her fingernails were thick and yellow. "An eldest, isn't she?"

The sun spilled over Elsie's shoulder straight into my eyes. "Yes, but—I've got to hurry, Mrs. Weather. I've got to go."

"Wait, Cruise girl." She reached forward and grabbed my hand. "How old is she, this Lindi?"

Her thumb bone pressed hard into my palm. I tried to pull away.

"How long till she goes to camp?"

"Mrs. Weather, I don't have time."

She pulled me toward her. Breathed into my face. I coughed.

"How old is she? How long till she goes to camp?"

It was Lindi's fourteenth birthday two nights ago. Everyone was there, even Elsie. *She can't have forgotten, can she?*

"She's fourteen. She's going on Saturday." I pulled my hand

away, right out of her grip. Her thumbnail scraped my skin. "I'm sorry, Mrs. Weather, I've got to go. I'm sorry."

"Storm's coming." She grabbed at me again.

I ran. Away from Elsie, away from the caravans, over to the town.

The Parker brothers were coming out of Frog Alley. Robbie, Neel, Grif, and Lyle, all thick beards and rolled-up sleeves.

"Help!" I called out. "Help! We need help!"

# Chapter 3

Robbie Parker knelt down and put his ear close to Lindi's mouth. Like she was whispering something he wanted to hear.

"She's breathing," said Jed. "Trig checked. Then he rolled her onto her side—"

"So she wouldn't choke," said Trig.

I squatted on the ground, not too close. Lindi's dress had green stains on it from the grass and red ones from her blood. They'd be a job to get out.

"You did well," Robbie said.

Was he talking to Trig? Jed? Me? He didn't take his eyes off Lindi. He slid an arm under her shoulder, pushing through her hair. His brother Neel cupped her head in his hands. Then Robbie tucked his other arm under her legs, rocked her toward him and stood up. Lindi hung pelt-like between his arms.

They carried her back across the cemetery—slowly, steadily—the way you'd walk if you were fetching mugs of milk that've been filled up too high.

"What were you lot doing all the way up here, anyway? Not making trouble, I hope?" Lyle Parker took a pair of glasses out of his shirt pocket and put them on. The glass bits—the bits you look through—were dark.

"No." We stared. How could he even see?

"Showing off your present from the mayor, Lyle?" said Grif. "Trying to impress a bunch of schoolkids? No stopping you, is there?"

"Shut up, Grif." Lyle looked at Jed. "You're an eldest, aren't you?"

"Yeah," said Jed.

"C'mon, then. Walk back with us."

They started off after the others.

They sang as they walked.

*In the northside fields where the daisies grow*
*I found my love, sweet Evie-oh*
*With her jet-black skin and her jet-black curls*
*Under the shadow of the gray willow."*

"Gray Willow." We'd heard it a million times before. The way the Parkers sang it, though, it was like it was a whole new song. Like it wasn't just a song—it was real. Maybe it wasn't really the Parkers singing at all. Maybe it was the dead relatives—William Whittington and Georgina Millicent Cruise and all the other dead Andersons and Cruises and Stanburys and Parkers—everyone who'd ever died and gotten buried in Fennis Wick cemetery.

They sang it soft and strong and dark and smooth.

*"She took off for camp with her billy lamp*
*Under the shadow of the gray willow."*

Me and Trig tagged behind, singing along under our breath.

~ ~ ~

The Parkers carried Lindi into Frog Alley. They disappeared between the houses, heading for Dr. Sunita's. Jed went with them, but me and Trig just sort of stopped at the entrance of the alley.

I scanned around for frogs, but there weren't any. A fat black caterpillar curled along the brickwork. I held my finger in front of it, but it wouldn't climb on. It arched its middle, wiggled round, and crawled along in the other direction. Slow as you like. *Funny how, somewhere inside it, there's the beginnings of wings.*

I prodded it. It fell off into the stinging nettles.

I looked back out toward the caravans. Elsie Weather was still there, kneeling down on her sponges in the strawberry beds.

It was extra quiet now. We couldn't hear the singing anymore.

I leaned against the wall. It was scratchy behind me. I pressed the back of my head into the bricks. *What would it be like if I cracked it against them really hard?*

*What would it be like if I got knocked unconscious, like Lindi?*

*What would it be like if I died?*

I closed my eyes and held my breath. *Would it feel like this?*

"D'you think Lindi'll be all right?" Trig flapped around the alley, all too-big hands and too-big feet. "D'you think Dr. Sunita can save her? D'you think Lyle can see out of those funny glasses?

He's so lucky the mayor gets him special presents. It didn't look like he could see out of them, did—"

He stopped still. His mouth went into a full-blown O shape.

"Oh no," he said. "Oh no!"

"What? What is it, Trig?"

"I left my sweater behind. My gray one. Up at the cemetery. Right near the tree."

"Oh, Trig. It's boiling. Why did you bring a sweater out, anyway? It's been boiling for weeks."

"Sorry." Trig stuck his hands into his pockets. His head dropped down between his shoulders. "I'll go and get it."

Mr. Wetheral's Siamese cat skulked past with a dead frog hanging out of its mouth.

"S'all right, Trig," I said. "You go home. I'll get the sweater. I'll be quicker."

He chucked his arms round me and squeezed. A proper Trig-hug.

~ ~ ~

The sweater wasn't there.

I went round the tree. I went round William Whittington and Georgina Millicent Cruise. I went round the whole blooming graveyard. It wasn't there.

Maybe he'd gotten mixed up. Maybe he'd left it somewhere else. Typical Trig.

*Just one last look behind the gravestones again.*

"Hey!"

*What was that?*

"Hey!"

It wasn't a shout. More of a really loud whisper.

"Hey!"

Yes. A loud whisper. Like whoever was saying it half wanted to be heard and half didn't.

"Here! Over here!"

It was coming from the hawthorn hedge. The boundary.

*Hedges don't whisper on their own. Hedges don't whisper unless someone's hiding on the other side of them.*

A head peeped out through the thinnest part of the greenery. A girl's head. With hair the exact same yellow as a pound-cake mixture right before you bake it.

I knew all the kids in our town. Been at school with them since I was knee-high. None of us had hair that color. And none of us would hide on the wrong side of a town boundary. Not ever.

She was a wanderer.

My heart paused.

My breath stopped.

*Dirty. Dangerous. Deceitful.*

"You looking for something?" She squeezed through the hedge and stood up all foal-like on long, skinny legs.

She was wearing a raggedy brown dress, a pair of rain boots that might have been red once, and Trig's gray sweater.

# Chapter 4

The girl grinned. There was a big gap between her two front teeth.

"Is she all right?" She tucked her pound-cake hair behind her ears. It fell straight back out again. "The one who fell out of the tree. Is she all right?"

She'd been watching us. All the time we were there.

"It's just you here now, isn't it? The others are gone?" she said.

I looked back toward the town. Too far away to see anyone. Too far away for anyone to hear a shout for help.

"You looking for this?" She pulled the front of the sweater away from her chest.

Mom'd go mad if we lost Trig's sweater. He'd only got two.

"I'm Una. Una Opal." She stuck out her hand.

I stepped backward.

"You can have your sweater," she said. "I'll give it to you."

She didn't take it off, though.

"I need some help first. That's all." She tucked her hair behind her ears again. It fell back out again. "I need you to get some food. For me and my dad. And antibiotics. He's got a bad leg, see? If you get me some food and some antibiotics, I'll give you your sweater."

I took another step backward and tripped over a gravestone. I scrabbled myself back to upright.

"Oh," she said, "are you okay?"

There was a look on her face, like she was worried about me. Worried I'd hurt myself. She wasn't, though. She couldn't be. She was a wanderer. It was just her being deceitful.

"I didn't mean to scare you," she said. "I just meant to— I don't know. Oh heck, I'm hopeless at this, aren't I?" She took a deep breath in and sighed it out again, big and loud.

"Here, just have the sweater." She grabbed it from the bottom and pulled it up over her head. She didn't hold it out or anything, though. She just twisted it in her dirty wanderer hands. "Will you still help me?"

The air was heavy. Hard to breathe.

"Or if you can't help me, just promise you won't tell anyone you saw me?" She clutched the sweater to her chest. Her eyes went shiny. Like when you're trying not to cry.

Did wanderers cry?

"Promise?" she said.

I nodded. Just a tiny bit. So tiny it wasn't even really a nod at all. And it didn't really count as a true promise, did it? Not if it was made to a wanderer.

She threw the sweater gently toward me. It landed on the ground between us. I darted forward, snatched it away, and ran as fast as I could back toward Anderson's field. I ran all the way to town for the second time that day. Didn't stop until I got to the vegetable plots.

I bent over and heaved in lungfuls of strawberry-sweet air. Had anyone seen me? Did they know what had happened?

No. There was no one around.

No one except Elsie, crouched down between the rhubarb leaves.

# Chapter 5

I crashed through the front door.

"Dad! Dad! Listen, I've just been—"

"Shush a minute, Magsie." Dad had peas and potatoes going on the stovetop. "I'm talking to Jed."

"But I—"

"Wait." He wiped his hands on a tea towel and hung it over his shoulder. "So, Jed—what happened when you got to Dr. Sunita's?"

"Yeah, what happened?" Trig was at the table with Jed, chin in his hands, eyes big as sunflower heads. "Is Lindi going to die? She looked dead when Robbie picked her up. Didn't she, Maggie? She looked dead. Completely dead."

"Course she's not going to die," said Jed. "She's fine. She started to come round when we got there, all by herself. Dr. Sunita said that was a good thing. Said she'll need lots of rest but she'll be okay to go to camp on Saturday."

Dad's face dropped. He looked old for a moment, like Grandad Cruise did after he'd got sick. Old and tired.

"What if she's not?" said Trig.

"What?" said Jed.

"What if Lindi's not all right to go to camp? What happens then? Has anyone ever been not all right enough? What happens then?"

"Shut up, Trig." Jed stood up. "She'll be fine." He put a hand on Dad's shoulder. "Dad? You okay?"

"Mmmm? Yes. Yes." Dad pulled up a smile. "Well, that's good, then. About Lindi being well enough for Saturday, I mean." He grabbed the potato pan and drained the water off. "But I bet she'll have a couple of supersized black eyes for a week or so."

"Yeah. I s'pose," said Jed.

"Actually"—Dad sploshed some milk into the pan, back to his normal self again—"I've got something for bruising in my medical bag. A good nurse is always prepared for these things." He threw me a wink. "Remind me after dinner, Jed—it's just there under the table. You can take her some tomorrow. Now, Maggie, Mom'll be home soon—could you mash these potatoes?" He passed me the pan.

"But, Dad, listen, I—"

"And Trig—can you set the table?" Dad shoved the masher along the countertop toward me.

"Why's it always me who has to set the table? Jed never has to do anything."

"Jed's an eldest." Dad passed Trig a fistful of cutlery. "Now, get on with it."

"Dad," I tried again. "There's something really important I've got to tell you—"

"Evening, all." Mom pushed in through the kitchen door, backpack first. "I'm starving."

"S'nearly ready," said Dad.

"Stop talking, everyone!" I said it louder than I meant to. Could they not just listen, though? Even for a moment?

They all looked at me.

"I saw a wanderer. A girl. Up at the cemetery." I twisted Trig's sweater in my hands, just like the girl had done.

"What are you talking about, Maggie?" Mom dropped her backpack onto the floor. She raked her fingers through her short dark hair.

"A wanderer. I saw one. In the cemetery."

"She's just being stupid." Jed rolled his eyes.

"I'm not!"

"We were all up there, Maggie," he said. "There weren't any wanderers. You're just trying to make yourself feel important because Lindi got all the attention today. Poor old Maggie-middler feeling ignored again."

"Really, Maggie, we don't have time for this kind of nonsense at the moment." Dad rubbed his forehead with the back of his hand. "We have to . . . I mean, Jed's off to . . ."

He trailed off.

"Dad's right." Mom touched a hand to his arm, then scooped a potato out of my saucepan and popped it into her mouth. "Jed's off to camp on Saturday, and there's his party to sort out for Friday. There's a lot of work to be done over the next few days."

"But you don't understand," I said. "I went back there, just me. And there was a wanderer. And she was wearing Trig's sweater." I held it up. "Is it even safe for him to wear it now?"

Jed smirked. "So, hold on," he said. "You're saying that there was a wanderer *inside the town boundary* and she was *wearing Trig's sweater?*"

"Yes! That's exactly what I'm saying. The mayor told us there were wanderers nearby, didn't she? Just this morning."

Dad laughed. "Nearby maybe, Magsie, but not inside the boundary. Wanderers might be dirty, but they're not stupid. Now, give Trig back his sweater, then get on and mash those potatoes. We don't have time for all your imaginings this week."

Mom picked another piece of potato out of the pan.

*No one believes a middler.*

*Not even their own mom and dad.*

It was all right for Jed, wasn't it? Everything was great if you were an eldest.

*Everyone listens to you.*

*You get to wear brand-new shoes and Grandad Cruise's old wristwatch and you sit around while everyone else does chores all day. Then you turn fourteen and you go to camp to lead a glorious life of fighting in the Quiet War.*

*Being special.*

*Being brave.*

*Being a hero.*

28

*While the rest of us are stuck in Fennis Wick forever, digging up potatoes and lugging barrels of water and doing never-ending piles of laundry.*

I chucked Trig his sweater and picked up the pan of potatoes. I pushed in the masher and pulled it back out again. *Shlup.*

*Shlup.*

*Shlup.*

*Shlup.*

Evidence. That's what I needed. Evidence that the wanderer girl was there. Then they'd have to believe me. Or better still, what if I actually caught her? If I caught her and brought her to Mayor Anderson, I'd be a hero too. Just like the eldests.

*Shlup.*

*Shlup.*

*Shlup.*

# Chapter 6

"Everyone finished eating?" said Dad.

I looked up. Everyone had finished except me. There wasn't any space in my head to be thinking about eating.

Was it dark suddenly?

Maybe I was just imagining it.

Dad started to gather up the dishes.

A snap of lightning flashed outside the window, whipped light across the table.

The storm. Elsie said there was one coming.

"Was that lightning?" Trig jumped up.

"Yep." Dad abandoned the dishes. "Maggie—get the lamps in, will you? Trig, help me with the blackout shades."

"I left the water on the cart." Mom brushed her hands together over her plate. "Better get it in."

"I'll help," said Jed.

Thunder rumbled through the house, through my chest, through my heart.

"Maggie—the lamps!"

Dad's shoes were on the mat by the back door. I slipped my

feet into them and flip-flapped out into the garden. Fat raindrops fell on my head. I gathered up all five billy lamps—Mom's, Dad's, Jed's, mine, and Trig's—and flip-flapped back inside.

Dad and Trig had done the downstairs shades and were clattering around upstairs. Mom and Jed were still out sorting the water.

So it was just me in the kitchen darkness. With Dad's medical bag underneath the table.

*Antibiotics.*

I turned on my lamp. The room filled with soft, warm, saved-up sunshine.

I grabbed the bag, unbuttoned it, and pulled the inside pocket wide. I picked out a small brown bottle, narrowed my eyes to read Dr. Sunita's tiny writing in the dim light. *Eshan Chowdhry. Cotellocene, 30 mg.* I put it back, picked out a second bottle. *Solly S. Pinner. Phenodicolyte, 10 mg.* Then a third. *Elsie P. Wetheral. Trellicillin, 250 mg.*

Trellicillin. That was an antibiotic, wasn't it? I had some once, for an ear infection. Elsie P. Wetheral—that was Elsie Weather's real name. We all called her Elsie Weather, though, on account of how she could predict the forecast. Or so she said. She'd been right about this storm for certain.

The bottle was hard and smooth between my fingers. It'd be stealing, if I took it.

"Shades are done! Lamps can go on!" Trig's feet *ker-lump*ed down the stairs.

I dropped the bottle into the bag and shoved it back under the table.

# Tuesday,
# September 2

# Chapter 7

Morning seeped round the edges of the blackout shades.

I scrunched up my eyes.

*Yesterday.*

*Lindi.*

*Crunck.*

*Trig's gray sweater.*

*Pound-cake hair.*

*Una.*

*The wanderer.*

*Dirty.*

*Dangerous.*

*Deceitful.*

*I could take her some food, steal her some medicine. Find out more about her. Get some evidence. Catch her, even. Turn her in and become a hero.*

*Or I could just keep quiet like I always do. And forget all about her.*

I got up and opened the shade. Another bright, hot day.

The storm had passed.

~ ~ ~

Miss Conteh beamed at us from behind her desk, enormous bags under her eyes.

"What a pleasure it was to read your summer diaries, Class Four."

She had two diaries clasped to her chest.

I beamed back at her.

"The person I've chosen to be runner-up has worked really hard on their diary. They've treated it with care, written some very interesting accounts of their summer activities, and drawn some beautiful pictures. I've read about fruit picking—"

*I wrote about that. I wrote about fruit picking.*

"I've read about long walks and seeing three rare red admirals up at the butterfly fields—"

*That was me too! We saw them on the last day of the holidays. I went home and wrote about it and drew the picture on the very last page.*

"And I've also read about making a birthday cake shaped like a hedgehog for someone's mom—"

*The hedgehog cake. Mom's birthday.*

My heart grew huge. It grew huge and it filled up my whole body. Miss Conteh was the best teacher in the world. The best teacher in the whole wide world.

"Yes, this year's runner-up is . . . Jed Cruise."

She held up the diary.

Bashed-up pages all different sizes and colors. Bent corners. Folded edges. A dirty old piece of string holding it together.

And nothing on the front except four words: *Jed Cruise's Summer Dairy*. Wasn't even spelled right.

How could he possibly be runner-up?

This wasn't a real competition at all. It wasn't about diaries. It wasn't about how well you'd done or how much work you'd put in. It was just like everything else in this stupid town. It was all about the eldests.

I ground my teeth together.

"Come on, Jed. Come up here. Let's have a round of applause."

Jed pushed his chair out. *Screeech*. He ambled to the front.

We all clapped for Jed. I made it look like I was clapping too, but I wasn't really. I slowed my hands down every time they came together so they didn't make any noise.

"And our winner," Miss Conteh went on, "is most deserved. I've never seen such a beautiful diary. Where did she even find the material that's been used to trim the edges? And these shiny little circles—are they sequins? Quite extraordinary. The winner of Best Summer Diary is Lindi Chowdhry, who sadly isn't able to be with us today as she took a rather large bump on the head yesterday afternoon. The good news, though, is that she's going to make a full recovery. Another round of applause, please, Class Four. You never know—if we clap loud enough, maybe Lindi will hear it from home."

Miss Conteh chuckled at her own funniness, and everyone clapped for Lindi.

Everyone except me.

I squeezed my fingers into my palms.

"Maddie?" Miss Conteh spotted me. She leaned forward. "Maddie Cruise? I'd like a round of applause from *everyone*, please. That includes you."

*Maddie.*

She still didn't even know my name.

"I hope you don't have a problem with my judging of the summer diaries?" she said.

I swallowed. "No, Miss Conteh."

She looked me right in the eye. "Our country is one of the few places in the world—perhaps the *only* place—that has kept the terrible enemy at bay during this war. Do you know why that is, Maddie?"

"It's Maggie. Not Maddie." I said it quiet. So no one could hear.

"Our geography has helped," she said, "and our land's wonderful capacity for self-sufficiency. But the real reason our country survives is *us*. Ourselves." She held her arms wide. "We are an adaptable people. Stoic, and brave. We understand the importance of hard work and sacrifice for a greater good, do we not? And our eldests, Maddie Cruise, are the bravest of us all."

Did she know what I'd been thinking? "Yes, Miss Conteh," I said.

She was right. Of course she was. It was right that Jed and Lindi won the prizes. They were eldests. They were going to camp, to keep the rest of us safe.

"So—a round of applause for Lindi. From *everyone* this time, please." Miss Conteh started a new clap.

*Our eldests are heroes. Our eldests are special. Our eldests are brave.* I joined in the clapping, properly this time.

"Now, Class Four," Miss Conteh leaned back and held down a yawn. "I want you to remember that *all* of your work was wonderful." She pushed the remaining pile of summer diaries to the front of her desk. "Could you hand them back please, Maddie?"

*Maddie Cruise.*

*Maddie-middler.*

*There's no point even trying, really, if you're a middler. No point even trying. Not unless you're prepared to do something as brave as the eldests. Like go to camp.*

*Or catch a wanderer.*

I put my chalk down on my slate. Pushed my chair out.

I was going to do it. For real. I'd start today. *Get home as soon as possible after school and take those antibiotics from Dad's bag.*

*Take them to the wanderer girl. Una.*

*Get her to trust me.*

*Catch her good and proper.*

*Then everyone'll remember my name, even if I am a middler.*

I walked over to Miss Conteh's desk. Was everyone looking at me? Did I look different now—now that I was going to be a wanderer catcher?

I picked up the diaries and turned round. Everyone was just sitting there, same as ever. Fidgeting, doodling, scratching, whispering. No one was looking at me. No one was taking any notice of me at all.

I handed out the diaries.

My stomach curled and twisted inside me.

~ ~ ~

We walked home across the square, the quickest way. I wanted to get back fast and find Dad's medical bag.

The sun grilled the backs of our necks.

"Maybe they were close, the diary competitions." Trig hadn't won a prize in his class either. He skittered around us, trying to keep up. "D'you think they were close? Maybe me or you would've got third place, Maggie, if there'd been a third place. D'you think me or Mags would've got a third place, Jed?"

"We weren't ever going to get first or second or third or fourth or even a hundredth, Trig. We weren't ever going to get anything."

"S'just a stupid diary competition." Jed kicked a stone. "Dunno what you're worried about."

A bunch of pigeons were strutting about in the middle of the square underneath the statue of Andrew Solsbury. They peckered around his cold stone feet. I didn't even bother going round them, just walked straight through. They flapped up, all in a panic. Some of them landed on Andrew Solsbury's shoulders. Some of them flew all the way up to the mayor's roof, the tallest house in town.

I looked up into Andrew Solsbury's face. I could never tell if he was smiling or frowning.

Trig stopped still. "What's going on over there?"

The mayor's house had a triangular gable over the front door. A huddle of people were gathered under it.

"What are they doing? Can we go and see? Can we, Jed? Can we, Maggie?"

"Let's just get home." I didn't have time for this. Had to get that bottle of trellicillin.

"But can't we go and have a look?" Trig hung back, stood on his tiptoes. "Just quickly?"

"Mayor's probably brought something back from the city," said Jed. "C'mon, Mags. We should go over. Mom won't be happy if we could've got something but didn't stop."

He was right, I s'posed.

We followed Trig over.

The mayor had a table set up in the doorway. It was piled high with blue gas canisters.

"Just one per household," she was saying. "These weren't easy to get hold of, I can assure you, and there's only a limited number. I'm ticking your names off the list as you take one, so no sending your kids back for another, all right? It won't work." She shoved a canister across the table to Figgie Rickard and ticked her name off the list. "Hello there, Trig. You going to take one for the family? Make sure you carry it straight home, won't you?"

"Yes, Mayor Anderson. I will. Straight home."

"What do you want for it?" said Jed.

"All I want, Mr. Cruise, is to help everyone through the winter." Mayor Anderson picked up a canister, leaving the handle free. "You ready for this Trig? It's heavy."

"I'm ready."

Trig grabbed the handle and the mayor let go.

*Smack.*

It dropped straight back down onto the table.

"Told you it was heavy."

"It's all right, it's all right. I can do it." Trig wrapped his arms round the canister and lifted it up in a Trig-hug.

*Fantastic.* It was going to take us ages to get home now.

"You'll never be able to carry that, Trig," I said. "Why don't we just leave it here and come back later with the handcart?"

"They might all be gone by then," said Jed. "Why don't I carry it?"

"No! I can do it!" Trig puffed out his cheeks.

He made it about twenty steps, then clanged the canister onto the ground. "I just need a bit of a rest," he said.

"Give it to me." Jed made a grab for the canister.

"No!" Trig pushed him away. "I'll do it. I'll do it." He got back up, gripped the handle with two fists and staggered on.

He got as far as the laundry.

"Oh, Trig," I said. "Told you we should've gone home first."

"Handcart." Mrs. Gebby was sitting outside the laundry like always, making sure people only went in on their proper allotted day of the week. "That's what you want. A handcart." She didn't even look up from her clickering needles. *Eyes in the back of her head*, Dad says.

Her brother, Frederick Parris, sat next to her in a wide-brim hat. His beard was flecked with ginger.

He blinked.

Frederick never says anything at all.

*He's helpful at the dairy*, Mom says.

*But he never speaks.*

*Not ever.*

*Not a single word.*

He had a book in his hand, with pictures of really old-fashioned people on the front. *Crime and* . . . something. It was upside down from where I was looking.

"S'all right, Mrs. Gebby," said Jed. "We're okay. I'll carry it from here, Trig." He picked the canister up like it was made of feathers.

Trig smiled at Frederick.

Frederick stared back.

"C'mon, Trig," said Jed.

"Yeah. C'mon." I grabbed Trig's arm. "Bye, Frederick. Bye, Mrs. Gebby."

Frederick carried on staring.

Mrs. Gebby carried on clickering.

Jed loped off toward home. Me and Trig scampered after him.

"Maggie?" Trig tugged on my sleeve. "Lindi says Frederick

used to speak when he was a littlest. Says he used to speak all the time. He never says anything now, though, does he? She says it's because he went outside the boundary. Is that true, Maggie? Is it true?"

"Shush!" I said. "Whispering's supposed to be quiet—not louder than how you usually talk." I glanced behind me. Didn't look like they'd heard.

"C'mon," Jed called over his shoulder. "Let's get home."

# Chapter 8

Mom was sitting at the table. Her feet were resting right on top of Dad's bag. Great. How was I going to get the antibiotics now?

Jed plonked the canister on the floor. "Gift from the mayor," he said. "One for each household."

"Excellent." Dad put it by the back door. "I'll tuck that away in the shed for emergencies. Blessed generator always breaks down when it's coldest."

"Mom!" Trig was the last in, just like always. He flung his arms round her. "You're never home this early."

"Mr. Wetheral's coming over." Mom hugged Trig back. "Didn't I tell you? Bringing Jed's portrait. I wanted to be here."

Jed's portrait. All the eldests had them done. Just the eldests, though. Not the youngests. And certainly not the middlers.

"Oh yeah." Jed pulled open the larder door and found the cookie jar. He popped the lid off and fished out a shortbread. "He said he'd bring it over before I leave for camp. Glad I don't have to go to his house anymore. Never been so bored in my life."

"Mr. Wetheral likes to spend a lot of time with his subjects."

Dad wiped the table with a dishcloth. "Helps him to capture the Real You."

"Couldn't he have captured it a bit quicker?" Jed sprayed crumbs out of his mouth.

I took a shortbread from the tin. Bit into it. Sweet and dry and buttery.

*I need you to get some food. For me and my dad.*

Would anyone notice if I took a few more?

*Knock-knock. Knock-knock.*

"That'll be Mr. Wetheral now. Get the door, will you, Magsie?"

~ ~ ~

Mr. Wetheral leaned on his stick. It made him look just like his mother, Elsie.

"Ah, the lovely Maggie. How delightful to see you." He held his hand out for shaking, his fingertips poking through the ends of his fingerless glove. He only ever wore one, on his right hand.

I shook it.

He smiled his uneven smile. The right side of his face, pulled and scarred, didn't work so well as the left.

*The whole right side of Mr. Wetheral got horribly burned in a terrible fire.*

Lindi told me. One break time, at school.

*It was wanderers that did it.*

*I can't believe you haven't heard this, Maggie.*

*He was with his family; they lived right on a boundary. And the wanderers—they set his house alight, with everyone still in it.*

46

*He had a wife, and two daughters. They died. All three of them. Mr. Wetheral tried to save them. He was all but dead himself when they dragged him out.*

*Someone my uncle knows was there. Saw it with his own eyes.*

*Screaming, they were. Screaming and weeping.*

"I, um, have your brother's portrait." Mr. Wetheral gestured toward the pony and cart behind him. It was Melissa, Mayor Anderson's piebald mare. Mr. Wetheral always borrowed her when he was delivering a portrait. His wife—the one who died—she was the mayor's little sister, so I s'posed she liked to help him out when she could.

"Is there any possibility I could have some help getting it inside?" he said.

I looked at his gloved hand, his scarred face.

Melissa swished a fly with her tail.

"Course," I said. "Course."

~ ~ ~

The portrait lay flat in the cart with a cloth pinned across its front.

"That's so you can uncover it yourselves," Mr. Wetheral said. "When you're ready."

We each took a corner of the frame, Dad and Mom and Jed and me. Dad didn't want Jed helping, but Mr. Wetheral said he should if he wanted to, so Dad gave in.

We hauled it off the cart. It was long and wide and heavy.

Melissa snorted and stamped a hoof.

"Is this bigger than usual?" I asked. My corner dropped lower than the other three. It was too heavy. Why was I breaking my

47

back heaving around a massive picture of Jed, just because he's an eldest?

"I make all the camp portraits exactly the same size," said Mr. Wetheral.

We edged it down the path, through the front door. We had to turn it on its side to get it into the sitting room. Trig scurried around in front making sure our way was clear. Mr. Wetheral followed us with his stick and his toolbox and his unsteady walk.

We propped it against the wall. The cover sagged. A sliver of dark green background showed along the top.

Mr. Wetheral pulled over a chair and took out a hand drill. He stood on the chair, held the drill firm to the wall with his strong arm, and wound it slowly with the weaker one.

We stood watching him—all five of us.

*All five of us.* If we were all in here, could I slip back into the kitchen? Take the antibiotics from Dad's bag? Maybe even get some of those shortbreads?

I took a sideways step toward the door.

"Oh, since you're here, Mr. Wetheral, could you do me a favor?" Dad dodged past me into the kitchen and carried on shouting through the doorway. "Would you take these antibiotics for your mother?"

He came back in with the bottle. The little brown bottle of trellicillin.

I should have been quicker.

"Of course. No problem at all. Put it next to my toolbox so I'll remember it."

"Great, thank you. Cup of tea?" Dad put the bottle down right in front of me.

My fingers itched to pick it up.

"A cup of tea would be lovely," said Mr. Wetheral.

~ ~ ~

We lifted the painting and eased it over the hooks. Nudged it till it was level.

"Would you like me to leave now? Give you some space?" Mr. Wetheral placed his empty teacup carefully into the saucer. We hardly ever used saucers, but I saw why Dad got them out. They seemed to suit Mr. Wetheral.

"No, no," said Mom. "Stay. We'd like you stay, wouldn't we?"

Mr. Wetheral looked at Jed. "What about you, Jed? Would you prefer me to stay or go?"

Jed shrugged. "Don't mind."

"In that case, I'll stay." Mr. Wetheral smiled. "Who's going to remove the cover?"

"Can I do it? Can I?" Trig jumped up and down.

Dad held the chair good and still, and Trig climbed up and pulled out the pins. The cloth dropped away.

I'd seen Mr. Wetheral's pictures before. Clear-as-life, full-body portraits of eldests gone to camp. Eyes that watch you so close you forget it isn't the real person right there in the room with you. Hands that might reach out any moment and pick a money spider out of your hair. All paid for with firewood or flour or a new right-handed, lovingly knitted fingerless glove.

But it was even more real when it was your own brother. Your own brother who you'd grown up with your whole life.

He was there. It was really Jed. Life-sized. Smiling that half smile he does, with his eyebrows just a little bit lifted, his lips just a little bit pursed.

The Real Jed.

Mom and Dad were all *Thank you, Mr. Wetheral*, and *It's remarkable, we don't know how you do it*, and Jed was all *Yeah, I guess it's a pretty good likeness but you guys see me a lot more than I do so you'll be the better judges*, and Trig was all *It's just like him, it's just like him, it's just exactly like him*.

But me? Nothing came out of my mouth at all. It wasn't just Jed himself; it was every part of the painting. The two roses carved into the top of the chair he was sitting on, curved and fine and wooden. The way Jed's feet dropped in toward each other, shoes resting heavy on the rug. And Grandad Cruise's watch—ten minutes past one exactly.

Jed was an eldest. It was good that we'd got the portrait done. It was right. But was anyone ever going to pay that much attention to me? Would anyone ever paint even a tiny picture of me?

"What do you think, Maggie?" Mr. Wetheral's question grappled its way through the other voices.

What did *I* think?

"Me?"

"Yes. I'd be interested to hear your opinion."

Why would he be interested in my opinion?

"Really?" I said.

"Yes, really. Do you like it?"

I looked again at the picture. The faded velvet curtains in the background. Jed's hair uneven on his forehead.

I didn't say yes. I didn't say no.

"It's like I can feel the solid petals of the roses," I said. "Like they're really wood, not just paint. And I can hear Grandad's watch ticking. And the dirt on the bottom of the shoes—that's real dirt, isn't it? And his hands . . ."

His hands. If I touched them, they'd be warm. They just would. For absolutely certain.

"But it makes me feel small," I said. "Like I don't count."

Mr. Wetheral nodded. He looked sad.

"Probably just because it's so big," I said.

He brushed some plaster dust from the front of his shirt. "Well," he said. "I'd better be off."

"Here." Dad picked up the trellicillin. "Don't forget this. Make sure your mom takes it three times a day, and that she finishes the whole bottle. Dr. Sunita's written it all on the label."

"Oh, thank you, that's wonderful." Mr. Wetheral tucked the bottle into his jacket pocket.

"Not at all," said Dad. "It's the least I can do. I mean, this portrait, if we didn't have it, I just don't know . . . I just don't know how we'd . . ." Dad ran out of words again. He pulled Jed toward him, scooped his head in close and nuzzled his hair. "My boy," he said, muffled.

Jed ducked away. "Dad!"

"What we're all trying to say," said Mom, "is thank you, Mr. Wetheral, for the wonderful portrait."

Mr. Wetheral went away with Melissa, leaving us with two Jeds and no antibiotics whatsoever.

~ ~ ~

Okay. If I couldn't get the medicine right now, I was going to have to refocus. On food.

The back door was open. Dad and Trig were outside getting the vegetables for dinner. Mom was feeding up the digester. The Real Jed was hanging on the wall in the sitting room, and the other one was nowhere to be seen.

I crept through the kitchen.

It was cool and dark in the larder cupboard. It smelled of cheese and lavender and hard-boiled eggs. The cold tiles felt good under my feet. I unhooked a cloth bag from the back of the door. If I just took a little bit of each thing, no one'd notice. I cut off chunks of cheddar, beetroot cake, homity pie. A handful of walnuts, a scoopful of oats. Two bread rolls. And four pieces of Dad's shortbread. Tucked it all into the bag. I slid out, through the kitchen, into the hallway, clutching the bag in front of me.

I pushed my feet into my shoes, then opened the front door carefully, so no one would hear the *click*. I closed it behind me, just as soft.

I headed for the cemetery.

# Chapter 9

I walked at first, so as not to draw attention. Down Frog Alley, through the strawberries, past the caravans. There was no one around. Just Elsie, pulling weeds. I took a wide path round her.

I got a bit faster. Swung the bag by my side.

Maggie Cruise.

Wanderer catcher.

Hero.

I ran across the mud ridges, toward Anderson's field.

My feet squidged into the earth where last night's rain had softened the ground. The whole world felt a bit less solid.

~ ~ ~

I sat down on William Whittington. He wouldn't mind. He was long dead. I put the bag down next to me.

A breeze shuffled the leaves.

Crickets chirped in the long, tickly grass.

The *clank, clank, clunk* of Mr. Gebby hammering horseshoes rang out from the town.

*Clank, clunk, clank.*

*Clunk, clank, clank.*

This was stupid. This was really stupid.

This was the stupidest thing I'd ever done in my whole life. What if it wasn't just Una with her sick dad? What if there was a whole army of wanderers out there? She could have been lying. Probably was, now I thought about it.

*I should go home. I should put everything back into the larder and—*

"Hey!"

My heart *gadump*ed.

"Over here!"

She sidled out from behind the tree—the same one Lindi had fallen from yesterday. Had she been there all the time?

"You alone?" she said.

I nodded.

She smiled her gappy smile. "I knew you'd come back. I knew you would."

~ ~ ~

I was going to have to speak. You can't gain a wanderer's trust without actually speaking to them. Trouble was, my brain had gone fuzzy and my mouth had dried up and my words had disappeared.

"What's your name?" she said.

*Maggie.* My lips made the right shape but no sound came out.

"Can't hear you." She grinned her gappy grin and cupped her hands behind her ears.

"Maggie," I croaked. "Maggie Cruise."

"Good to meet you, Maggie Cruise." She stuck out her hand.

She was taller than me. A whole head taller. I clasped my hands to my chest.

"S'all right." She dropped her arm down. "We don't have to shake hands. Bit old-fashioned anyway. Let's wiggle ears instead."

She stood right in front of me and lifted up the sides of her hair.

"Ready?" she said.

One step closer and we'd have been touching noses. My heart kicked at my rib cage. What would Jed do? What would Lindi do? What would any of the brave eldests do?

*No idea.*

"Ready," I whispered.

"Here goes, then."

She stared right at me and her ears wiggled up and down. All by themselves. Without anything else moving at all.

"Your turn," she said.

I didn't need to hold my hair up. Mom cut it short, first day of every month. *Long hair just gets in the way.*

I clamped my teeth together and wiggled. My whole face crunched and scrunched but my ears stayed completely still.

Una grinned. "Hard, isn't it? Hold on, watch this."

She lifted one ear, and then the other, changing sides. Left, right, left, right, left, right.

*Wow.*

"How d'you do it?" My voice came out normal.

"My grandad taught me." She dropped her hair back down.

"He said most people think it's genetic. Most people think you're born so that you can either do it or you can't, and nothing can change it. They're wrong, though. You can learn. Anyone can. You just gotta know how. Want me to show you?"

Her grin again. That gap between her front teeth.

I pressed my tongue against the back of my own front teeth. They were tight together. No space at all.

"Yes," I said. "Yes, please." I held out the bag. "This is for you. And your dad."

She took it, and our fingers touched. Wanderer skin.

Strange. It felt just like normal.

She looked inside.

"There's no antibiotics," I said. "Not yet. I think I can get some, though. My dad's a nurse."

Her eyes glistened with tears again, like they did yesterday. "This is so kind, Maggie," she said. "I'm so lucky I met you. Thank you. Thank you."

I shrugged. "S'okay."

"C'mon, let's go over there, behind those walls." She set off alongside the hawthorn, toward the old church. "We'll be well hidden. I'll give you your first lesson in ear wiggling."

I took a deep breath and followed.

~ ~ ~

We squashed down some grass to sit on, near where the newer gravestones were. There were the three Wetheral graves, all in a tidy row. Not overgrown like the others, but clean and neat and tended.

She put her fingers on either side of my head, just above my ears. "There are little muscles up here. Can you feel them?"

*I shouldn't be here. I shouldn't be talking to her. I shouldn't be letting her touch me. She's dirty.*

But running away wasn't going to make me a hero, was it?

"Kind of," I said.

"Everyone's got them, we're just not used to using them. Try and move my fingers. Go on—try."

My shoulders moved. My eyes moved. My mouth and my nose moved. Everything moved apart from the bits I was supposed to be moving.

"I can't."

"Course you can. You just need to practice, that's all. Here, put your fingers where mine are—that's it—then try and move them. Do a little bit every day. The muscles'll get stronger."

I tried again, with my own fingers there this time. Still didn't work.

We sat back against the wall.

"How old are you, Maggie?"

"Eleven," I said. "How about you?"

"'Bout the same, I s'pose." She pulled up a long piece of grass, twisted it round her fingers. "My dad doesn't take much notice of stuff like that, so I'm not too sure."

Not too sure? How could you not know how old you are?

"Have you got a birthday?" she said.

"Course. Fifteenth of November. Everyone's got a birthday."

"I haven't. I'd like one, though. Hey—maybe mine could be

the fifteenth of November too." She tucked her hair behind her ear. It fell straight back out. "S'months away, though. Maybe I'll make it sooner. How about this week?"

"It's my brother's birthday this week. Friday."

"Well, I'll have mine on Saturday, then. No, Sunday. Leave a day in between. Yes. It'll be my birthday on Sunday and I'll be eleven, just like you."

We had our legs stuck out in front of us. Una's were way longer than mine—more like twelve-year-old legs than eleven-year-old ones. Maybe even thirteen. She tapped the toes of her rain boots together while she talked.

"Can we meet up here," she said, "me and you? On Sunday? We could, y'know . . . do whatever it is you do on birthdays."

I s'pose you wouldn't know what you do on birthdays, not if you've never had one.

"Yeah," I said. "Yeah, all right."

She wanted to see me again.

I was doing it. Me, Maggie-middler.

I was catching a wanderer.

She wasn't what I expected, though. She was dirty, for certain. Mud caked into the creases in her knees and black crescents under all of her fingernails. She didn't have my mom coming at her with a hard brush and a bar of carbolic soap every Sunday night, that's for sure.

But she didn't seem very dangerous.

"Maggie?" Una picked up the bag. "D'you mind if I go now? I'll give you another ear-wiggling lesson another day, I promise

I will. It's just that my dad, he's really hungry. I'd like to get this food back to him."

"Oh. Yeah. Course."

"It's been fun, though." She stood up and brushed off her dirty dress. "It's ages since I had any friends."

*Friends?*

"And don't worry about the ear wiggling. Takes a lot of practice. Took me a full month before I got anywhere at all. If you've got a mirror, use that."

She slung the bag over her shoulder.

*No more hesitating, Maggie-middler. No more waiting. Find out where she's living. Find out right now.*

"I'll, um, bring more food," I said. "Where can I, um . . ." My throat clogged up. I coughed. I tried again. "Where can I find you? I mean, where are you living?"

"We're stopped up in a barn," she said, pointing somewhere vaguely beyond the boundary.

Beyond the boundary? No way could I go beyond the boundary.

"But you'll never find it," she said. "Just come here, to the cemetery. I'll find you."

"Oh. Okay."

"You won't bring anyone else, will you?"

"No. Not if you don't want me to."

"I don't." She wasn't grinning anymore. Her face was still.

*No more hesitating, Maggie. No more hesitating.*

"Why not?" I said.

She sucked her lips between her teeth, looked at the ground. "People in towns can be dangerous sometimes, that's all."

*Us? Dangerous?*

"If we're so dangerous," I said, "why are you here?"

"I really need help. My dad's hurt his leg and he's getting a fever and he can't hunt. He can't even travel, which is why we're stuck at the barn. We're so hungry. And when I saw you help that girl, the one who fell out of the tree, I figured you and those boys—"

"Jed and Trig. They're my brothers."

"Yeah, you and your brothers, you seemed different. The sort of people who might help."

I picked at the skin on the side of my thumbnail.

"Thanks so much for this, Maggie." Una patted the bag. "You're the best. I'll bring your bag back. Promise. Will you come again soon? Sooner than Sunday?"

"Yeah. Okay."

She squeezed through the thinnest part of the hawthorn hedge. Beyond the boundary. The grass looked brighter out there. Fresher.

Maybe it was just the sun.

"Bye, Maggie." She clonked away from the boundary in her almost-red rain boots, through the brighter, fresher grass. When she reached the forest, the brown of her dress and the yellow of her hair merged into the branches till I couldn't tell what was Una anymore, and what was trees.

I sat down on William Whittington, chin in hands, elbows

on knees. I'd done it. I'd met with a wanderer. And I was going to see her again.

Mr. Gebby *clank*ed and *clunk*ed. The crickets *buzz*ed and *click*ed and hopped.

The breeze shuffled the leaves: dead relatives whispering in their graves. Whispering and watching.

# Wednesday,
# September 3

# Chapter 10

Trig was bent over the kitchen table, his hand curled all the way round his pencil. Dad's medical bag was right next to his feet.

*There must be some more antibiotics in there now. Can't be only Elsie who needs them.*

Trig didn't get his work done in time at school again. His teacher had found him a piece of furry-edged paper and a stubby pencil so he could finish it at home. So here he was, writing out Andrew Solsbury's eldest edict in his very best handwriting. Taking ages. I could've done it a thousand times over by the time he'd reached the end of the first line.

*From this day forth every eldest child, at age fourteen, will be awarded the privilege of attending military camp.*

I didn't blame Trig for taking so long, though. Probably would've been quicker if they'd picked something more interesting than an old politician's speech from a million years ago. Like a poem or something? A song?

I sat on the end of the table with my feet on a chair. Put my fingers either side of my head. Tried to wiggle my ears.

*Lack of strength, intellect or character will be no barrier.*
*Each one of them will fight for country and glory in*
*    this terrible war.*
*Their childhoods will be joyous; and a peaceful life*
*    is guaranteed for the rest of the family, who from*
*    now on will not see the war, nor hear it, nor touch it.*
*It will become the invisible war, the quiet war.*
*I call on you to support those who support the edict*
*    and punish those who do not.*
*Shame upon any who refuse to send their eldests to*
*    camp.*
*Shame upon them and their kin.*

Trig finally finished. Weird thing was, he had the worst handwriting out of all of us if you made him hurry up, but if you gave him as much time as he wanted, it was beautiful. All ups and downs and tails and loops.

It always made his hand ache, though. He flopped his wrist in front of me.

"It hurts, Maggie. It hurts."

"S'all right. You've finished now. Nice job too. Why don't you go and help Dad outside? He's doing something with the zucchini. Want me to put this in a safe place?"

"Thanks, Maggie." He ran out. "Dad! Dad! I finished my handwriting!"

I hooked the medical bag out from under the table with my foot. Pulled it open. Rooted around inside.

Nothing.

No bottles at all.

Not even ones that weren't antibiotics.

Not even after all that waiting.

I shoved it back under the table.

I took Trig's writing into the sitting room and put it on a shelf. The Real Jed's eyes followed me across the room. I saw something at the bottom right corner of the painting. I stepped closer.

*Jed G. Cruise, Eldest Bound for Glory.*

*H. S. Wetheral.*

I walked backward into the kitchen with Jed's eyes following me all the way. I shut the door after me.

~ ~ ~

"So." Mom dropped her backpack onto the table. Bits of dried mud fell off it and scattered everywhere. "It's Jed's party on Friday. We're going to need some help getting things ready."

"Me and Maggie never get a party." Trig pressed his fingernail into a piece of the mud, making even more mess. "Why can't we have parties too?"

"Jed's an eldest."

Dad came over with a wet cloth, but Mom swooped an arm

across the table before he got there. Pushed all the mud onto the floor. I caught Dad's eye. He winked.

"There's a lot to do," said Mom. "First things first. Trig, would you go over to the Wetherals' after dinner and get a forecast from Elsie? I don't want to be using the town hall if I don't have to."

*Elsie?*

"Why do I have to go?" said Trig. "It's Jed's party, so he should go, shouldn't he? Jed never has to do anything."

*Elsie Weather?*

"Mom's asking *you*, Trig," said Dad.

*Elsie Weather, who—for absolutely certain—has got a bottle of trellicillin in her house?*

"But I don't like going to see Elsie. She never smiles. I keep watching her to see if she'll smile, but she never does. Not even—"

"I'll go." They all looked at me. "I'll go, and Trig can do whatever you were going to ask me to do. That all right?"

"I don't care who does what, as long as it gets done." Mom roughed up her hair. It stood up on its ends. "Take her some cheese, Maggie, for payment."

"Not cheese." Dad picked up a dish of new potatoes from the countertop. "Flour. Take a jugful of flour."

"All right, then." Mom swiped a potato from the dish. "Cheese *and* flour."

Trig gave me a huge, great Trig-hug. "Thanks, Maggie."

"That means you're making pastry dough with Dad after dinner, Trig," said Mom. "A *lot* of pastry dough."

Trig slumped into a chair. "But I hate making pastry dough."

"Tough," she said.

~ ~ ~

I lifted the woodpecker door knocker. Tapped its head forward so it pecked the door. *Peck-peck-peck.*

The Siamese cat crept up. Gave a snarly meow.

I knocked again. *Peck-peck-peck.*

The cat blinked.

*PECK-PECK-PECK.* I knocked harder.

The door opened and the cat shot inside.

"All right, all right. Give an old woman a chance to get down the stairs." It was Elsie, leaning on her stick. Dressed in the exact same red-and-white-checked dress I have to wear to school. *Must be a hundred years, though, since she was a schoolgirl.*

"Um, I was wondering, Mrs. Weather, if I could get a forecast?"

Her eyes went to the jug.

"Flour." I held it up. "I've brought flour for you. And cheese."

"Forecast?"

I nodded. She opened the door wider. I stepped inside. She closed the door behind me and the hall went dark, only a grimy bit of light leaking in through a high window. My eyes took a moment to adjust.

The hall had piles of things all down one side. Coats, odd shoes, stacks of books—even heaps of paper. More paper than I'd ever seen in one single place. I glanced over it all, checking for the little brown bottle.

"Um, Mom says——"

"Quiet, Cruise girl, Hannard's got a sitting."

The door to Mr. Wetheral's painting room was ever so slightly open. A slice of someone——a girl, I think——was just visible through the gap. Mr. Wetheral's soft voice murmured in the background.

Elsie held out her free hand for the cheese. She unwrapped a corner and sniffed it. Slipped it into her apron pocket. Held her hand out again. I passed her the flour.

"In there." She pointed with the jug to the back room. "I'll get tea."

"Oh no, Mrs. Weather, it's——"

"Quiet, girl. In there."

Trig was right. She didn't ever smile.

The back room was packed full of all kinds of junk. A jumble of boxes and crates and pots and bowls; mugs with the handles broken off; olden-day cables with plugs on the end that fit into the wall; boards with the whole alphabet written on them in little squares. *All useless*, Dad'd say. And there were books. Piles and piles of books. Some on shelves that went right up to the ceiling. Ten times as many as in the whole school library.

I picked my way between the stuff. Sat down on a half-empty chair, moved a glass off the seat. LA ANGELS, it said on the side of it.

On the wall in front of me hung old photographs and certificates and little wooden carvings and even two long, thin masks that had straw for hair and empty spaces where the eyes should be. Everything was ancient and crooked and squashed together.

I bent forward and lifted the flap on a cardboard box—it was full of yellowy printed paper. Newspapers from the old days.

SHAME UPON THEM read a thick black sentence across the top paper. The rest of the writing was smaller. *A family was driven out of Midleaf by angry neighbors last week when they defied the eldest edict and refused to send their son to camp.*

*Driven out?*

I pulled back some of the papers and read another one further down the pile. TOGETHER WE CAN SAVE OUR COUNTRY. *Andrew Solsbury, leader of the opposition, speaks a message of hope. Will it win him next week's snap election?*

I looked at another even further down. DARK TIMES ARE UPON US. *A series of coordinated world-wide terrorist attacks have—*

"Cruise girl?"

I dropped the papers and sat up.

"Tea." Elsie shuffled through the door with a sloshing mug.

I stepped back through the junk and took the mug. I sniffed it. Chamomile. Yuck. "Thank you, Mrs. Weather."

Elsie made her way across the room with her stick. She stopped to wheeze after each step.

"Can I help?" I said. "Shall I clear a path for you?"

"Don't touch anything. It's Hannard's."

Maybe to Mr. Wetheral this stuff wasn't junk at all. Maybe it was treasure.

I sipped at my tea. If I sipped at it enough times, I'd get to the bottom eventually.

Elsie reached the glass doors at the back. "What do you want to know, then, Cruise girl? Forecast for Halloween? Christmas? Hundred percent right. Every time. Nature doesn't lie. Doesn't have the capacity."

"Just Friday, please, Mrs. Weather. My mom wants to know whether it'll rain on Friday. Jed'll be fourteen, see? It's his party."

She grunted, struggled with the key for a moment, and opened the door.

The garden looked even messier than the house. Overgrown vegetables, clambering ivy, sprawling shrubs, shadowy trees. Plants and leaves creeping, climbing over everything.

Elsie prodded with her stick, found firm ground, and stepped out.

"Wait there," she said.

She wobbled across the weed-woven patio, somehow managing to stay upright. Then she waded into the undergrowth in search of insects to pinch and seed heads to break open.

I didn't have long.

I crept back out into the hall. Mr. Wetheral couldn't see me from this angle. I looked over the piles of coats and shoes and books—no sign of any medicine bottles. Checked in between the stacks of paper, quiet as you like. Still no medicine.

*Where else could it be? Think, Maggie. Where would Dad keep ours?* I looked around.

The kitchen.

It was as chaotic as the rest of the house. Worse, maybe. Water barrels and a potato bin just sitting there in the middle of the floor. Wonky piles of crockery and an overflowing compost box on the countertop, the Siamese cat curling in and out of them.

And over by the back window—a table.

Definitely the sort of place you might put a bottle of medicine.

I balanced my mug on the end of the counter and went to investigate.

The table was completely covered. Bits of cutlery, old coins going green, orange-handled screwdrivers, an empty vase with a dark ring round its inside. Books, glasses, mugs, a hacksaw—and there, at the edge, a small brown medicine bottle. The trellicillin.

There was a window behind the table. Elsie was still in the garden, turning over leaves and squeezing grubs.

I picked up the bottle. *Elsie P. Wetheral. Trellicillin, 250 mg.* Still almost full.

I looked back to check that Mr. Wetheral and his visitor were still in the front room—and stopped dead.

# Chapter 11

Mr. Wetheral dropped out of my mind. Elsie dropped out of my mind. Even the trellicillin dropped out of my mind.

Three paintings. On my left. On the kitchen wall.

I stared.

They were smaller than the usual portraits—just the head and shoulders. One was of a woman and the other two were girls, one a bit older than me, one a bit younger. Half of each face was as lifelike as any of Mr. Wetheral's paintings: lips that would squash under your finger if you pressed them, curled hair as deep and dark as burnt jam.

But the other half of each face was all wrong. The younger girl's was patterned and criss-crossed and patchworked: the face of a rag doll. The older girl's melted into the background of the painting: ear, hair and skin blending into the wall behind her. The woman's face just stopped: a sharp line down the middle of her head so all you could see was the carved-oak pattern on the back of her chair.

One side of each face was damaged, just like one side of Mr. Wetheral's face had been damaged by the fire.

*He had a wife, and two daughters.*

*Screaming, they were.*

*Screaming and weeping.*

I lifted my hands and touched my eyes, my nose, my mouth.

Soft. Smooth. Even.

*It was wanderers that did it. They set his house alight.*

Wanderers.

Una?

Her dad?

Could they really have done something like that?

*CRASH!*

My mug shattered on the floor—tea all over the place, the cat right above it on the countertop.

I stuffed the bottle into my shorts pocket.

The cat glared.

"Mother? Is everything all right?" Mr. Wetheral came out of the painting room with his uneven steps. Strong foot, weak foot, strong foot, weak foot.

"Mr. Wetheral, I—"

"Ah—Maggie Cruise." He made his way through the hall. "I thought I heard someone at the door earlier. What was the crash? Is Mother okay?"

"She's fine, yes. She's in the garden. I'm just here for a forecast. The crash—it was my mug, and the cat. I'm sorry. Shall I clear it up?"

Mr. Wetheral looked at the three portraits, then back at me.

"Maggie?" Beth Goodman came out of the painting room. An eldest, due for camp in a few months.

"What are you doing here, Maggie?" she said from the hallway. "You shouldn't be here, you're a middler. Mr. Wetheral only paints eldests. Isn't that right, Mr. Wetheral?"

"Well, that's not exactly how I'd—"

"I'm not doing anything," I said. "I mean, I just came for a forecast, for Jed's party, and Mrs. Weather gave me a cup of tea, and I came into the kitchen to put the mug back and then the cat knocked it off the side. I'm sorry, Mr. Wetheral. I'll clear it up. Have you got a cloth? And a broom?"

"It's okay, Maggie. Don't worry. It's not your fault." Mr. Wetheral's voice was soft and calm. "Beth—go and get yourself settled again, I won't be long."

I cupped my hand over the bottle-shaped lump in my pocket.

*Got to get out, Maggie. Got to get out.*

"Cruise girl? Cruise girl? You still here?" Elsie shuffled in from the back room.

"Careful, Mother," said Mr. Wetheral, "there's a broken mug on the floor."

"Yes, I'm sorry, Mrs. Weather, it was an accident."

Elsie came into the kitchen and steered herself round the broken mug, hardly even looking at it. She opened a cupboard and pulled out a bundle of something—something wrapped up in a tea towel, with four corners tied tight and neat on top.

"Scones." She held it out with a shaky arm.

"Thank you, Mrs. Weather, but I'm not hungry. I just came for the—"

"To share." Elsie nodded at the trembling bundle.

"To share? Who with?" The bottle pressed against my leg.

*Got to get out.*

*Got to get out.*

"You'll think of someone, I'm sure."

"Take them, Maggie," said Mr. Wetheral. "Mother bakes the best scones in town."

"But, Mrs. Weather, what about the forecast? For Friday—Jed's party." I took the bundle from her, one hand still firm over my pocket.

"Forecast?" Elsie rubbed her bony fingers across her lips. "It'll be sunny, Friday. Watch out Saturday afternoon, though." She fixed me in the eye. "Everything's changing, Saturday afternoon."

~ ~ ~

I ran down the path. The bottle bulged in my pocket. I was no good at this stealing thing. No good at it at all.

I skidded round the corner, eyes on the ground—

*OOF!*

I got flung back, but whoever I'd bumped into had me by the arm and kept me upright.

"In a hurry, Maggie?"

Mayor Anderson.

"Not getting yourself into trouble, I hope?" She kept ahold of my arm. The skin on her face had tiny red veins all over it. "What's that you've got there?

The trellicillin?

How did she know about it?

Could she see it through my pocket?

"I said what's that, Maggie?" She nodded at the tea-towel bundle.

The scones.

Course she couldn't see the trellicillin. Course she couldn't.

"Oh, that. It's just some scones. From Mrs. Weather."

"I see." She let go of my arm. "You all right, Maggie? You seem a bit jumpy."

"No, Mayor Anderson. I mean, yes, I mean—" *I should tell her.* About Una and her dad. After all, they're wanderers, and look what the wanderers had done—they'd killed Mr. Wetheral's whole family. "The thing is, on Monday I—"

Hold on.

I didn't have any evidence yet.

She wouldn't believe me.

And Una's dad hadn't got the antibiotics. He was still sick. It wouldn't be fair to hand him in just yet.

And I sort of wanted my second ear-wiggling lesson too.

"I mean, yes, Mayor Anderson. I'm fine. I was just, um, running up to the butterfly fields. Trig left his sweater there."

It was all I could think of.

"Youngests, eh? Hopeless." She winked. Smiled her upside-down smile. "Listen up, Maggie. Tell your mother I'll have something for her on Saturday, after I've taken your Jed to camp. I've been promised some bananas. First time ever. I'll be setting some aside for her."

"Oh, okay. Thank you."

"Thank you, what?"

"Thank you, Mayor Anderson."

"S'more like it. Go on then, get off after your brother's sweater."

I skidded away in the direction of the butterfly fields. Not the right way for the cemetery, but I'd cut across, once no one was looking.

I touched my pocket as I ran.

Bottle was still there.

*What did Mayor Anderson say she was bringing back on Saturday?*

*Bananas?*

Those yellow things.

I'd seen pictures of them in books.

# Chapter 12

I peered through the thinnest part of the hawthorn, its tight red berries hanging close to my cheeks. The forest spread out beyond.

"Una? You here?" I did that loud whispering thing, so Una might hear but it wouldn't carry far. "Una?"

"Here. Over here." Just five rulers away from me Una emerged out of the hawthorn—like she'd magicked herself up from the leaves and the branches. She tucked her hair behind her ears. It fell straight back out—again. You'd've thought she'd stop bothering to tuck it back in the first place by now.

She smiled, but only a small one. "I knew you'd come, Maggie." Her eyes were red. Wet.

"You okay?" I said.

"Yeah, course." Her mouth moved into a grin shape, and her gap showed and everything, but it wasn't a proper smile.

"You don't seem okay," I said.

She took a wobbly breath in. "It's my dad. He's worse. Much worse. He's not even making sense today. And the wound on his leg, it kind of . . . smells bad. And we're stuck out here and there aren't any other wanderers nearby, and I don't like to leave him for too long. I don't know what to do, Maggie; I just don't know what to do."

The trellicillin.

I pulled the bottle from my shorts pocket. "Here, I got this."

Una took it. "Is this antibiotics?"

"Yeah. For your dad. It'll help his leg. And his fever."

Una's mouth dropped wide open. She held her hand to her lips. "Oh. Oh. I can't believe it. I never thought . . . I can't believe it. Maggie, are you even real? You're like our guardian angel!"

I picked at my thumb.

Una turned the bottle so the label was on top. "Who's this, though?" she said. "Elsie P. Wetheral? Is this her medicine? Will she be okay without it?"

*Will Elsie be okay?*

I hadn't even thought about that.

"She'll, um, she'll be fine," I said. "She'll just think she lost it. Or never had it in the first place. Her memory's not so good, see. She can get another bottle. Dr. Sunita's got plenty more."

Did Dr. Sunita have plenty more? I didn't know.

Una shook her head. "I can't believe it. You're the best, Maggie Cruise. The best. Is it really okay? Can I really take them?"

"Course."

She put the bottle into the big patch pocket on the front of her dress and pulled out the cloth bag from yesterday.

"Here," she said. "This is yours. The food was delicious. DEE. LISH. USS. Dad wasn't up to eating much, so I've saved some for him. Oh, it was the best food I've eaten since he hurt his leg. In fact that homity pie was probably the best thing I've eaten since Grandad died. Dad's fine at hunting, but he's not a great cook, and neither am I."

*Since Grandad died?*

"When did your grandad die?" I said.

She bit her lip. "Winter before last."

Winter before last. Water froze up in the laundry pipes that year. We had to help Mom dig cows out of the snow. They didn't all get dug out alive.

"It was really cold," I said.

"Yep. Too cold for an old man to survive, that's what Dad said."

I remember. Mayor Anderson gathered up all our old folk that winter, and anyone with babies. She put them up in the town hall and kept a fire going the whole time, even at night. Got the Parker brothers to make everyone a hot meal every day, and porridge in the mornings. Grandad Cruise loved it. *Cuddling babies and singing songs all day—what more could you want?* he said.

Must've been hard to be a wanderer that winter.

"What was he like, your grandad?" I said.

"He was the best grandad ever." Una grinned. "Taught me how to ear wiggle. And he used to make us poached eggs with wood garlic whenever we could get our hands on eggs. And when Dad went night-hunting, he used to stay with me the whole time playing card games—blackjack or gin rummy. I used to get so tired the cards all dropped out of my hands."

My heart squeezed in my chest. For Una. For her grandad. But most of all it squeezed for Grandad Cruise. He survived that winter, but he died all the same a few months after.

"My grandad died too," I said. "Last year."

"He did?"

"Yeah."

"Of the cold?"

I shook my head. "His heart. It got worse and worse and worse till he wasn't really properly Grandad Cruise anymore. He used to take us fishing, before he got sick. Made us nets with old curtains and sticks. But that all stopped when he got ill, and then he died, and there was no more Grandad Cruise at all."

Una stuck her hands in her pocket. Fiddled with the bottle.

"They're still here in a way, though, aren't they? In our minds." She patted the top of her head. "In our memories. If we remember them, they're not completely gone. That's what I think."

She was right. Grandad Cruise wasn't completely gone. Not while I still remembered him.

"Have you practiced your ear wiggling?" she said.

"A bit." I tried a wiggle. "Still can't do it, though."

Una looked back, past the hawthorn, toward the forest.

"D'you mind," she said, "if we save your second lesson for another day? It's my dad. He's so bad. I don't want to leave him for long."

"Course," I said. "You should go, take him the antibiotics."

"Will you come again? Tomorrow, maybe?"

I nodded. "Tomorrow. After school. I'll bring more food, if I can."

*Food?*

The tea-towel bundle.

I had a whole load of scones with me—right now.

I held them out. "You can have these too," I said. "Scones. I nearly forgot."

"Are you sure?"

"Course."

I didn't need them.

Una scooped up the bundle in both arms. "You really are our guardian angel, Maggie."

She slipped through the hedge, out of Fennis Wick. I peered after her, through the thorny, berried branches. She walked across the grass and merged into the forest.

A breeze rippled through the hawthorn. Something tiny caught my eye. A chrysalis, swaying, suspended under a leaf. A brand-new butterfly inside. All wrapped up and thinking itself safe, but hanging by only the tiniest thread.

~ ~ ~

It was late. I pulled down the blackout shades and got undressed, but I didn't get into bed. I sat up against my pillow, knees tucked under my nightshirt.

Food.

Had to get Una some more food.

To catch her. Not to help her.

She was a wanderer. Dirty, dangerous, deceitful.

I wasn't doing this to help her.

Not really.

I practiced wiggling my ears while I waited for everyone else to go to sleep.

When it was quiet, I turned on my billy lamp. It glowed warm in the darkness. I picked it up and crept out of my room.

Shadows loomed on the walls as I padded down the stairs. Quietly, quietly, quietly.

*Eeeeeeek.* Why did the kitchen door squeak so loud at night? Hardly noticed it at all during the day. Funny how your hearing gets better at night but your seeing gets worse. I lifted the lamp a bit higher.

*Sniff, sniff.*

I stopped. Was that someone in the sitting room?

*Sniff.*

I let a little light through the doorway. Someone *was* there, curled up in an armchair, crying. Right in front of Jed's portrait.

*Mom?*

Mom didn't curl up. Mom didn't cry.

Mom dug up potatoes and shouted at dairy cows and trod muddy boots over clean kitchen floors.

She didn't curl up and cry.

"Mom?"

She jerked up.

"Maggie? You made me jump. What are doing down here?" She looked away, hiding her face.

"Just getting some water." My eyes were getting used to the dimness. I could see some of the Real Jed. His hands. His face.

"It's a wonderful portrait, isn't it?" Mom cleared her throat, smoothed down her nightshirt. "We're lucky. Mr. Wetheral has done us proud. Yes, we're very lucky. Brave Jed is off to camp on Saturday, and we've got a wonderful portrait to keep. We couldn't be any luckier."

"Are you all right, Mom?"

*What do you do when your mom cries?*

*Hug her?*

*Say something?*

I just stayed in the doorway.

"Yes, yes," she said. "I'm fine. I'm going to miss him, that's all. Jed. I'm going to miss him when he goes to camp. And I've been thinking about Lil too, and all the things we used to do together."

"But Lil's doing okay, isn't she?" Lil. Mom's big sister who went to camp years ago. A commander in the Quiet War now, too busy to visit.

"Mmmm? Oh—yes. Yes, she's doing fine. I just miss her. And I'll miss Jed."

"But it's good that he's going to camp, Mom. He's an eldest. Special. Brave."

"Course it is, Magsie. Course it is. Absolutely right."

"And we'll see him when he gets back."

She cleared her throat again. "Yup. Yup. Course we will."

"And maybe Lil'll be able to come and visit us one day."

"Yup. Yup. I'm sure that's right." She pushed her hands through her hair. "Well, I'm off to bed now. Hurry up. Get some sleep. School in the morning."

She climbed up the stairs into the darkness.

No wonder Lil never came back to visit. If I got out of Fennis Wick and didn't have to spend the rest of my life scrubbing laundry and lugging water and making pastry dough, I wouldn't ever come back either.

I went through the kitchen, into the larder. Breathed in the cheese and the lavender.

I filled up the bag, took it upstairs and hid it in my middle drawer. No one ever looked in there. I'd take it over to the cemetery after school tomorrow.

To catch Una.

Not to help her.

# Thursday,
# September 4

# Chapter 13

"Maggie?"

Mom's voice reached into my sleep.

"Maggie?"

I opened itchy, smudgy eyes.

"You awake, Maggie?" she called from the landing. "Better get up or you'll be late for school."

School. I had to sit through a whole 'nother day of school before I could take Una's food to the cemetery.

I pulled the covers back over my head.

~ ~ ~

"You'll all be pleased to hear that Lindi Chowdhry is well enough to be with us this morning." Miss Conteh blinked like she wasn't properly awake yet. "But we only have her until lunchtime. Dr. Sunita wants her to get plenty of rest, what with her going to camp this Saturday. Isn't that right, Lindi?"

"Yes, Miss Conteh." Lindi sat up all prim. She had a dotted pink scarf wrapped round her head, tied neat at the nape of her neck. She'd have been as tidy and proper as always if it weren't for the dark purple hoops around her eyes. She looked like the Parker brothers after too much home brew and a midnight brawling.

"I've been hearing a little more about Lindi's accident." Miss Conteh stifled her third yawn of the day. We'd only been in class for fifteen minutes.

"It seems," she carried on, "that Jed Cruise, another of our eldests, bravely administered first aid and was constantly at Lindi's side until help arrived, showing us again how valuable all our eldests are."

*Bravely administered first aid?*

It was Trig who remembered the first aid—all of it. And help wouldn't have arrived at all if I hadn't run all that way to get it.

"Well done, Jed," Miss Conteh went on, "and congratulations on your speedy recovery, Lindi. I'm sure only an eldest would have the capacity to heal so quickly. I hope my little Michael will grow up just the same."

Lindi tilted her head toward Jed. His cheeks reddened.

No point in saying anything. No point in saying anything at all. No one'd listen. Not yet, anyway. Not till I was a hero. Which was what I was going to be, as soon as I'd caught a wanderer.

Soon as I'd caught Una.

Which I was definitely going to do, once her dad got better.

And then everybody'd start listening.

"Now, Class Four, I'm sure I can rely on you to be very careful around Lindi this morning. No pushing or shoving, and if she shows any signs of being ill, please let me know immediately."

At break time everyone wanted to hang round Lindi.

"Can I see your stitches?"

"Did Dr. Sunita save you?"

"Did Jed give you the kiss of life?"

"Jed *kissed* you?"

"Did you actually die and come back to life?"

"Ugh. Did you wake up with Jed's mouth all over you? Ugh."

"I *nearly* died." Lindi looked at them all from under her dark eyelashes. "Jed saved me. In fact, if it wasn't for him knowing all that first aid, I probably would've died for sure."

She twirled a piece of hair that had escaped from under her headscarf.

Trig started jogging on the spot, which is what Dad told him to do when he starts feeling panicky.

Jed opened his mouth like he was going to say something, then closed it again.

"Come on, Trig," he said, catching my eye.

We both took one of Trig's arms and led him off to the other side of the playground. We sat down on the hot pavement. I pulled at the chickweed growing up between the cracks.

"It's good that Lindi's all right, isn't it?" said Trig, legs still jittery.

"Yeah." Jed wiped his nose on the back of his hand.

"Yeah," I said.

"It was me who remembered the first aid, wasn't it? Wasn't it, Jed? Wasn't it, Maggie?"

"Yeah. It was you."

"Course it was."

I pulled more chickweed.

How long'd it take to pull all the chickweed in the whole playground?

A day?

A week?

Jed brushed his hands over the ground. Picked up a stone.

"Did you hear what Beth Goodman said yesterday break-time?" said Trig. "Did you hear, Maggie? Did you hear, Jed?" He picked at his top lip. "She said Mayor Anderson forgot to pull down her blackout shades the other night. Said her mom had to go round and knock on the mayor's door to remind her. And Beth said her mom said if Mayor Anderson keeps forgetting we're all going to get blown to smithereens in the middle of the night and it'll all be the mayor's fault. D'you think she'll forget again? D'you think we'll all end up in smithereens? What are smithereens? Jed? Maggie?"

"Stop fretting, Trig." Jed flicked his stone across the crumbling pavement. "I'm sure she won't forget again." He flicked a second stone.

Trig found a piece of broken pavement and flicked that. It didn't go as far as Jed's. The two of them dropped onto their stomachs and had a flicking contest.

I looked out southward. Beyond the cemetery. Beyond the boundary. Trees and hills and bushes, sizzling in the sun. Somewhere, hidden away, there was a barn. With Una and her sick dad inside.

Unless she was lying, of course.

Which she could be.

But I didn't think she was.

Only four and a half hours of school left.

Only four and a half hours till I saw her again.

# Chapter 14

"Hello, Maggie. It's not often I see anyone up here in the cemetery on a Thursday evening."

Mr. Wetheral. What was he doing here?

He walked toward me, stick in one hand and a pair of shears in the other. Strong foot, weak foot. Strong foot, weak foot.

"Um, hello, Mr. Wetheral." I threw a sideways look at the hawthorn. Was Una there? Had he seen her? "I, um, just like to come up here sometimes. To, er, see the butterflies."

"The butterflies?" He lifted an eyebrow. "Wouldn't you be better off going to the butterfly fields?"

Yup, I would. If butterflies was what I was really looking for.

"Well," he said, "I'm sure you get plenty of butterflies over here too. Lots of stinging nettles round the old church, and as Mother says, *Where there's stinging nettles, there's caterbugs*."

I glanced behind the tree. *Stay hidden, Una, if you're here. Stay hidden.*

"I've been trimming the graves." Mr. Wetheral held up the shears.

"The graves?"

I looked at William Whittington and Georgina Millicent Cruise. They seemed as overgrown as ever.

"My family. They're at the back of the church."

The Wetheral graves. Of course. Neat and tidy and tended.

"Oh," I said. "Yes."

"Well, I'd better be off. You enjoy your butterflies. Look— there's one now."

A cabbage white fluttered up from the long grass.

"Goodbye, Maggie."

"Bye, Mr. Wetheral."

I ran behind the tree and slid down beside it until my heart stopped galloping.

"Hey!" That loud whisper. Una.

"Is he gone?" She climbed out from the hawthorn. She had a grin on her face this evening. Gappy and huge and . . . smeared with purple.

Blackberries.

"Yes, he's—"

"You'll never guess what, Maggie! This is the best day ever. It's my dad—those antibiotics are making him better already. After only one day! You saved his life, Maggie. You saved his life!" She grabbed me with purple-stained fingers and swung me round. The bag of food flew round with us.

"Shh!" I laughed. "Shhh! People'll hear us!"

"And guess what else I found?" she said.

"A blackberry bush?"

She stopped swinging. "How did you know?"

I grabbed her purple hands and turned them palms up. "You're covered in them."

Una's laugh was the funniest laugh ever. Snorty and honky, both at the same time. It made me laugh too, just hearing it.

"Oh, Maggie, you've got to come and meet my dad, come and see for yourself. He's talking and making sense and everything. He's going to be all right and it's all because of you. Come with me and see him."

She pulled me over toward the hawthorn.

I pulled back. "I can't," I said.

"It won't take long; we're not so far away—"

"No, it's not that. It's the boundary. I can't go beyond the boundary."

"The boundary?"

"The hedge."

We both looked at the hawthorn.

"You mean you're not meant to go past it?" she said.

"Course I'm not. No one is."

"I haven't been to a town with a boundary before. *Boun-dreee.*" She said the word slowly. Like it was a new one she'd just learned. "There's no one around, though, is there? Who's to know?"

*I'd* know.

Even if no one saw me, even if I didn't get caught, it'd be

there in my head and it'd never go away. It was bad enough stealing the antibiotics. Going past a boundary was way worse.

"And so what if anyone *does* know?" she said. "S'not exactly murder, is it? Come on."

She pulled on my arm.

I pulled back. "Frederick Parris got locked up for going outside the Leap Cross boundary."

"Locked up?"

"That's what Lindi said. He got caught and was locked up for years and years and years, and when he came out he never spoke again. Not a word. He just reads his books now. And helps out at the dairy sometimes. Never says a word."

"They locked him up just for going out of town?"

"Going past a boundary. It's dangerous. Puts the whole of Fennis Wick at risk. There are wanderers out there—I mean, um, I mean, there are dangerous people out there." *Shut up, Maggie, shut up.*

Una grinned a purple smile. "You mean dangerous people like me?"

"No, I didn't mean that, I—"

"Weird, isn't it, how *you* think there are dangerous people *outside* your town, but *we* think there are dangerous people *inside* it."

It was kind of weird, now she put it like that.

The bag handle was pressing into the soft bit of my fingers. I pulled it up onto my shoulder.

Una frowned at the hawthorn. "My dad told me not to get too

close to your town. *It's an unknown quantity*, that's what he said, but he never mentioned anything about boundaries. So how d'you know this particular hedge is a boundary? Just looks like any old hedge to me."

*Any old hedge?* Was she joking?

"I mean, how d'you tell the difference between a *boundary* hedge and an ordinary one?"

"Well, it's all in the song, isn't it?" I said.

"The song?"

"Y'know. The boundary song."

"The boundary song?"

"You don't know the boundary song?"

She stared at me.

"Are you spinning me up?" I said. "It's the first song anyone ever learns. Devvy Chowdhry was singing it before he could crawl. He was a late crawler, mind."

"Well, good for Devvy Chowdhry. I'm not spinning you up—I don't know it. I'm not from round here. I never learned it."

*S'pose she's right. You wouldn't know it, would you? Not if you hadn't grown up here.*

"Sing it for me, Maggie, go on."

"Sing it? On my own?" I was going to look like a complete la-la singing the boundary song on my own out here in the cemetery.

"Yeah, go on, I want to hear it. Please?"

She was serious. She really did want to hear it.

"Well, okay. It goes like this, um . . ." I took a breath. *"Hello there, dear partner, how are you this morning?—"* But Una was grinning now and I fell into giggles.

"Don't stop!" said Una. "I know the tune! It's the same as 'The Ash Grove.' Grandad used to sing it to me. *Down yonder green valley, where streamlets meander.*" She sang the words. "See? It's the same! Don't stop, Maggie."

"All right, all right, I'll try again." I swallowed. *"Hello there, dear partner, how are . . .* Hold on, do you want me to do the actions too?"

"There are actions? Of course I want the actions!"

"Okay, okay, you'll have to be my partner, so you stand there." I dropped the bag of food into the grass, got hold of Una's shoulders, and positioned her in front of me. "You have to imagine there are loads of us and we're making two circles, one inside the other—oh, it'll all make sense in a minute."

"It will?" Una stood with her hands by her sides, all straight and upright and awkward. I fell into giggles all over again. How could she not know this?

"Sing me the song!"

"Okay, okay. So the first thing we do is bow, like this. *Hello there, dear partner, how are you this morning?* Then we shake hands. *We'll sing all the boundaries, shake hands, then move on.*"

"All right, all right." Una blew on her hands and rubbed them together like she was going for a tricky catch. "Let's do that again so I've got it."

We bowed and shook hands all over again. Then we went through the whole song with all the actions.

> "Hello there, dear partner, how are you this morning?
> We'll sing all the boundaries, shake hands, then
>   move on.

> The edge of the marshes right up to the river;
> the mill and the wheat fields will keep you in line."

We splodged our feet in imaginary marshes and waved our fingers like the wheat.

> "Along Conker Alley and down into Leap Cross,
> then follow the hawthorn along past the church."

We did the leap and triangled our arms into the church shape.

> "The fence passing South View and leading to
>   Disdale,
> then keep in the crescent and all will be well."

We held our hands to our foreheads to shield out the South View sun. We drew the crescent in the air.

> "I thank you, dear partner, for sharing the boundaries
> but now I must leave you and wish you good day."

We shook hands and stepped to the side to meet our new partner who wasn't actually there because there were only two of us.

We did it again and again. Una kept doing a church shape when she should have been shielding out the sun and wiggling her fingers when she should have been splodging her feet.

I laughed so much I got a stitch in my side. "Stop! Stop! It hurts too much!"

"Bring your knee up."

"What?"

"Bring your knee up. Like this. It'll make your stitch go away." She stood on one leg and pulled her other knee to her chest. "S'a proven cure. Works every time." She hopped around on her one leg.

I pulled up my knee and fell over.

Una snorted and honked and fell over too.

We lay on the grass and looked up at the sky.

Clouds, light as cobwebs, strung in the blue.

"What's it like, being a wanderer?" I said.

"What's it like? It's just normal. It's all I've ever been. There aren't any boundaries."

The clouds drifted. Slowly, slowly, slowly.

"What's it like living in your town?" she said.

"S'all right."

*There are boundaries, for sure.*

*Plenty.*

*But they're to keep us safe, aren't they?*

*No one starves if they can't hunt.*

*And everyone's got a proper house to live in.*

*Chirp, chirp, chirp.*

The crickets were still out.

The sun was hot on my face.

"You could just poke your head and shoulders through," said Una.

"Poke my head and shoulders through what?"

"Through the hawthorn."

"Just my head and shoulders?"

"Yeah. That's not the same as going beyond it, is it?"

She was right. That wasn't the same as going beyond it. It wasn't the same at all.

~ ~ ~

The hedge didn't seem like a hedge anymore. It seemed like a brick wall.

"I can't, Una. I can't do it."

"Sure you can. It's easy as anything. It's just the same on that side as it is here."

I looked back toward Fennis Wick. No one could see this far. Mr. Gebby's hammer rang out a few clanks.

Una pulled back some spiky branches. There was the brighter, fresher grass.

"S'easy, look." She stuck her head through, then pulled it back out. "Your turn."

My mouth was dry.

I clenched my fists.

I pushed through the brick wall—hands, head, neck, shoulders. The hawthorn clung to my arms to keep me from leaving. It clawed at my skin.

I was there. On the other side of the boundary. Sort of. The air smelled of grass and red apples. I breathed it in. It slithered down my throat, a swirl of outside drawn into my lungs. I looked round for the apple trees, but there weren't any.

"See?" said Una. "It's just the same."

I took another breath. My head swooped with the green and the red and the brightness and the freshness. I pulled it back into Fennis Wick and collapsed on the ground, heart thundering.

"No, it's not," I laughed. "It's completely different."

Una honked and snorted.

My head began to steady.

"Una?" I sat on the grass in front of her. The sun was sinking behind the hawthorn.

"Yeah?"

"What about your mom? Is your mom in the barn too?"

She stopped laughing. "No," she said. "She died when I was little."

She *died*?

"Oh. I, um, I'm sorry, I—"

"S'all right. It was a long time ago." She looked right at me, but her eyes weren't really focused properly. She was picturing something else—or some*one* else, most likely—and I'd gone see-through.

"Did she get sick?" I said.

"No. She got too close to an unfriendly town."

"An unfriendly town?"

"Some towns are friendly. They'll trade with us, give my dad a bit of work sometimes. Others, well, others just don't like wanderers at all. Even now." Una's eyes stayed unfocused. "We hadn't eaten in a while, Dad says. She crept off while we were sleeping, to find some food. She knew he'd never let her go if he was awake."

"What happened?"

Una shrugged. "She never came back. That's all."

"I . . . I'm sorry . . . I didn't . . ."

"Don't apologize. Wasn't your fault." Her jaw hardened. "Thing is, you have to be careful when you're a wanderer. And she wasn't careful enough."

I picked at the grass. "Do you remember much about her?"

Una shrugged again. "Don't remember what she looked like, or what she sounded like or anything. She's just a sort of shadow, picking me up, setting me down. Shooing a fox from me once—I think I remember it. Or maybe I just heard about it from Grandad. Anyway," she smiled a little, "it's fine. We're okay, me and my dad. We're fine. Especially with you helping us now."

I smiled back.

"Hey." She grabbed my hand and pulled me up. "Will you come again tomorrow, Maggie? Please come."

Tomorrow. September fifth. Jed's birthday, and still a million things to do for the party. No way Mom was going to let me get away.

"Can't come tomorrow. But I'll come Saturday, and Sunday too. For your birthday."

"My birthday! I nearly forgot. My first proper birthday."

"I'll bring cake," I promised.

**Friday,**
**September 5**

# Chapter 15

The bedsheets were wrapped round my legs.

I untwisted them, pushed them off.

My skin was damp and sweaty.

I blinked.

Opened my eyes properly.

Fifth of September.

Jed's birthday.

"Maggie! Trig!" Mom shouted up the stairs. "I'm keeping you both home from school today. I need your help for the party."

Great.

A whole day of preparing for Jed's party. Because he's an eldest.

It was good. It was right. It was proper.

Jed's an eldest. Special and brave.

Spending my whole day getting stuff ready for his party was the right thing to do.

But what if . . . What if I could do whatever I wanted today?

What would I do, if it was just up to me?

I'd visit Una. Spend all day with her, wiggling ears and talking and singing the boundary song.

And sticking my head and shoulders through the hawthorn.

Maybe going all the way through.

Lying on brighter, fresher grass, looking up at the sky.

No I wouldn't.

That was stupid.

Course I wouldn't.

Wanderers were dirty and dangerous and deceitful.

I was only spending time with Una so I could catch her.

No. I'd go up to the butterfly fields. With some paper. A whole clear sheet of paper. Crisp and new. And pencils. Colored ones.

That's what I'd do.

Draw painted ladies and peacocks and cabbage whites, and more red admirals if I was lucky enough to see one.

It'd be more fun if Una came too, though.

We could make a picture together.

"Maggie!" Mom again. "Are you up yet? There's so much to do."

I got out of bed. Pulled up the blackout shades.

I went over to my tiny mirror for some ear-wiggling practice. All the stuff that needed doing would have to wait just a little bit longer.

~ ~ ~

Five o'clock. My feet ached from being on them all day. My hands ached from beating eggs and kneading dough and crushing mint and slicing bread. My back ached from lugging chairs and tables and huge, tottery stacks of plates. My nose itched from all the toadflax and bellflowers we'd picked and trimmed and jarred up for the tables.

*Don't worry, Maggie. One day everyone else will be running round, beating and lugging and itching for you.*

*Maggie the wanderer catcher.*

*Maggie the hero.*

I sat down in front of the Real Jed. The other Jed, home from school now, peeped under the tea towels at all the plates of food we'd prepared.

"Is this . . . It is! Goldie pie, my favorite—can I have some?" He didn't wait for an answer. Just scooped up the largest piece and took a crumbly, syrupy mouthful.

I rolled sideways and rested my heavy head on the chair arm.

"It was a great day at school today, Mags," he said with his mouth stuffed full. "Because there's two of us going to camp tomorrow we hardly did any real work at all. All we did was . . ."

My eyelids sank. Jed's voice drooped and drawled in my ears. I disappeared into deep-red swirling sleepiness—

*Knock-knock-knock.*

My eyes popped back open.

"That'll be the first guests arriving," Dad called out from the kitchen. "Maggie, answer the door, would you? And leave it on the latch."

~ ~ ~

It was Elsie Weather and Mr. Wetheral. Of all the people I hoped wouldn't arrive first, here they were. It was impossible

113

to even look at Elsie without thinking about the stolen bottle of trellicillin.

"Hello, Mr. Wetheral, Mrs. Weather. Would you like to come in?"

"Good evening, Maggie. Sorry we're so early." Mr. Wetheral ushered Elsie into the house. "Mother likes to get a seat."

I opened the door wider. My fingers remembered the hard, cold feel of the stolen bottle. My leg remembered the shape of it in my shorts pocket.

"In here." I showed them through to the sitting room. "Would you like a drink? There's Dad's home brew, or some raspberry-ade?"

A few more people arrived while I was getting the drinks. Mrs. Zimmerman and her family, some Parkers, and some Stanburys.

I carried two glasses of raspberry-ade to Mr. Wetheral and Elsie.

I couldn't look them in the eye so I gazed down instead. Elsie's knees curled over the edge of the chair. They had wide brown spots on them from the sunshine.

Mr. Wetheral propped his stick up and took the drinks. One bare hand, one gloved.

"Splendid," he said. "Splendid."

"Okay, well, I'd better go and—"

"Hold on a moment." He passed a glass to Elsie. She wrapped both hands round it, as if it was hot tea.

"I'd like to ask you something, Maggie," he said.

*Here goes, then.* I was in for it now. They must have figured out it was me who stole the antibiotics. A big lump appeared in my throat, about the same size and shape as a little brown medicine bottle. I gulped it down.

"I was wondering whether you'd considered what you might like to do when you leave school."

What I might like to do when I leave school? What had that got to do with anything?

He took a sip from his glass.

"I, um, don't know," I said. "It's ages yet. I'll work in the fields, I s'pose."

"Is that what you want to do?"

*What I want to do?* Funny question.

"S'what most people do, isn't it?" I said. "If you're not an eldest."

He took another sip.

I licked my dry lips.

"You don't want to be a nurse, like your dad?"

I looked round. No sign of Dad.

"Can't think of anything I'd rather be less," I said. "All those sick people. Don't tell him I said that, though, will you?"

Mr. Wetheral leaned forward. "It'll be our secret," he whispered. "Well, ours and Mother's."

Elsie's eyes were closed. Was she asleep? The glass tilted in her hands.

"I was wondering," he said, "and please feel free to say no if it's not what you want—but I was wondering if you would consider becoming my apprentice."

His apprentice?

Could you even be an apprentice portrait painter? I'd heard of a blacksmith apprenticeship with Mr. Gebby, or an apprenticeship up at the tannery, but portrait painting? I must've heard him wrong.

"Becoming your what, Mr. Wetheral?"

"My apprentice. I'd teach you to become a portrait artist. We could start putting a little groundwork in while you're still at school."

"But, I—"

"I've seen your work, Maggie." He placed his glass on the floor. Rubbed the back of his gloved hand. "I asked Mrs. Zimmerman to show me the artwork of all the children in the top half of the school. I've done my research."

"But I'm not the best at art, Mr. Wetheral. Susi D'Vere is much better at—"

"I looked at *all* the artwork. Even Susi D'Vere's." He placed his hands on his knees. "I chose you. Do you think it's something you might like to consider?"

"Um, yes. Yes. Yes. But are you sure?"

"I'm in absolutely no doubt at all, Maggie. It's not just about drawing or painting or shading, you understand. One can learn all of those things. It's about *seeing*. And you, Maggie Cruise, have a good eye. You see things. You're, um . . ." He looked up to the ceiling, "*special*. Yes. That's the word."

"Maggie? Maggie!" Dad called from the kitchen. "I need some help with this cake."

Special. Mr. Wetheral thought I was special. My palms were wet. I wiped them on my shorts. "Thank you, Mr. Wetheral. But I don't need to consider it. I'd like to be your apprentice. I'd like that very much."

"Well, I'm delighted." Mr. Wetheral smiled his uneven smile and sat back in his chair. "I think we'll get along together splendidly."

"I'd better go and help Dad now," I said.

Mr. Wetheral's apprentice. I was going to be Mr. Wetheral's apprentice. Painting pictures for a living. Not ploughing up fields or shouting at the dairy herd.

Maggie Cruise—portrait painter.

Maybe life in Fennis Wick wouldn't be so bad after all.

~ ~ ~

The walls groaned with so many people crammed into the house. Tables creaked under piles of food. Sweat glistened and slipped and stank. The happy-sad songs of the Rickard sisters' violins threaded through the chatter and curled across the ceilings.

Everyone was here. The whole town, pretty much. There wasn't any proper air in the house anymore, just a big cloud of everyone else's breathed-out breath. I took bigger and bigger lungfuls just to try and get any oxygen at all.

*"Maggie, could you take this to . . ."*

*"Maggie, have you got a . . ."*

*"Maggie, where can I find . . ."*

*"Maggie, I need you to . . ."*

But it was all right.

Everything was going to be all right.

All I had to do was get through this party, see Jed off tomorrow, and then I could go and find Una again. Una, outside, beyond the boundary. Clonking around in her almost-red rain boots. Breathing in the trees and the brighter, fresher grass.

And after that, when I finished school, I was going to be Mr. Wetheral's apprentice. A portrait painter.

But wait. If I was going to be a portrait painter, did I really need to be a wanderer catcher too?

Couldn't I keep things as they were? With Una as my secret friend?

I gathered up an armful of empty plates from the sitting room and weaved through to the kitchen. The floor was sticky under my shoes. It was going to need a whole lot of cleaning up afterward.

Mom and Dad were over by the back door. I could just see them between the heads and shoulders of everyone else. Dad's face was buried in Mom's neck, her arms wrapped round him.

*Great. Them just standing there getting all hugged up while Maggie-middler does all the work.*

I squeezed over to the counter and dumped the plates down. Heaved in another breath.

"Oh!"

Trig bashed into me and sloshed raspberry-ade all down my leg.

"Trig!"

"Sorry, Maggie, it wasn't my fault; someone pushed me. I

couldn't help it. I'm sorry." He peered into his glass and puffed his cheeks out. "And now all my drink's gone on the floor."

I took the glass off him. "C'mon."

We made our way over to the jugs and I poured him another raspberry-ade. He gulped it down.

"Wanna go outside, Trig? I can't breathe in here anymore."

We squished between bodies, into the hall and out the front door. The air was still thick and heavy but it was better than inside. There were people spilling onto the street and down the road. A bunch of littlests dodged in between our legs.

"Let's find Jed," I said.

We found him in next door's garden. Lindi was walking along the dividing wall, heel to toe, heel to toe. She had a half-eaten slice of Dad's beetroot cake in one hand and no headscarf on. Her hair bounced past her shoulders in shiny coils and her black eyes had gone from purple to yellow.

"Hi, Jed! Hi, Lindi!"

Me and Trig climbed onto the wall and dangled our feet over the side.

Jed was frowning up at Lindi. "I'm just saying, are you really sure you should be up there after what happened on Monday?" he said. "What if you fall off?"

"I can do whatever I like, Jed Cruise." Heel to toe, heel to toe. "I'm an eldest, in case you hadn't noticed. Just like you. And we can do whatever the heck we want."

"I know, I know, I was just thinking that—"

"Well, you can stop thinking. You can stop thinking right now and come over here and kiss me." Lindi swayed a little, like grass in a breeze. "Well? What are you waiting for? Come on." She jumped down and put the cake on the wall.

Jed looked at me. I bit my lips between my teeth.

"We should have kissed ages ago. We've wasted so much time." She stepped closer to Jed.

"Do you like the beetroot cake, Lindi?" Trig hopped down and pushed himself between the two of them. "Dad says it's his best ever. Aren't you going to eat that bit? Can I have it if you don't want it?"

"Get out of the way, Trig. I'm trying to kiss your brother." She shoved Trig to the side.

"Don't push him." My voice was louder than I expected.

"What?" Lindi was as surprised as me.

"Don't push him. You think you can do whatever you want just because you're an eldest, but you can't. Don't push him."

"Tell your middler sister to shut up, will you, Jed? Tell her to go back to her normal mousy self."

"Lindi, don't." Jed reached for her hand but she twisted away.

"Don't? I told you, Jed, I can do whatever I like, and I can say whatever I like."

"No." I jumped off the wall. "No, you can't. You eldests, you're all the same. Just because you were born first, everyone thinks you're so special. Well, I don't. Not anymore. I'm going to be just as special as you. I'm going to be Mr. Wetheral's apprentice—he asked me earlier on."

Lindi shoved her face in front of mine. "You don't know what you're talking about, middler. You don't know how easy you've got it."

Easy?

*Easy?*

I stood myself up tall. Tall as I could go.

"Easy?" I said. "You eldests get everything—big parties, the best clothes, you win all the prizes, you get praise for stuff you didn't do, we even chant about you every day in assembly—"

"And you'd swap places, would you? Rather be an eldest? Have a good think before you answer, middler. Would you rather know that as soon as you turn fourteen you'll be taken away from everyone you've ever known? Sent to camp? To train for war? Where people are going to kill you if you don't manage to kill them first? You'd swap your middler place for that, would you?"

The war. She was talking about the Quiet War.

I never really thought much about the war.

*I s'pose I might, though, if I was an eldest.*

"And I don't care what the mayor tells us," she said, her nose close to mine, her breath damp on my face, "or what our parents or our uncles or our aunts tell us—I don't know anyone who's ever come home from the war—do you?"

*Anyone who's ever come home?*

*Well, there's . . . there's . . . I don't know. Can't think. Can't speak.*

"Swap your middler place for that, would you?"

Trig started jogging on the spot.

Jed tried to take Lindi's hand again. She pushed him away, but he was stronger. He wrapped his arms round her, pulled her toward him.

"It'll be okay, Lindi," he said. "We're going together. I'll stay with you."

And right in front of us Lindi's face crinkled up and she started to cry.

"Go away, Maggie," said Jed.

"But I—"

"Just go away."

He pulled Lindi over to the wall and they slid down it, crouched on the ground, all bundled up with each other. Lindi sobbed into his shoulder.

Trig stared at them.

"HOI! HOI! HOI! HOI!"

It was the Parker brothers, building up for a juggle.

Lindi kept sobbing.

Jed kept hugging.

Trig kept staring.

"Let's go watch the juggling, Trig." I pulled his arm. He was stuck to the spot.

"Come on." I yanked him away. "Let's go."

~ ~ ~

Trig and me found our way to the front of the crowd. The Parker brothers were there, leading the clapping and whooping. Trig joined in, but my hands wouldn't clap and my mouth wouldn't whoop. I just kept seeing Lindi and Jed in my head, crouched by the wall, sobbing and hugging.

*You'll be taken away from everyone you've ever known.*

Robbie Parker disappeared round the back and reappeared with two axes, a pitchfork, and a spade. Must've raided Dad's shed. He threw the spade and axes to his brothers. They caught them with sure hands and spaced themselves out across the road. Everyone took a step back. We'd all seen the Parker brothers juggle before. They were good, but not as good as they thought they were.

Garden tools tumbled in the darkening air. The sun dipped down behind the houses.

*People are going to kill you if you don't manage to kill them first.*

Spikes and blades and shovels spun upward and somersaulted down into the brothers' hands.

*You'd swap your middler place for that, would you?*

The crowd whooped and *ooooh*ed and spilled its drinks and dropped its food.

*You don't know how easy you've got it.*

After a bit, Grif got cocky. He turned to wink at Hilary Sundae and missed a catch. The crowd scattered like spooked pigeons. The only person who didn't move was Mayor Anderson. The pitchfork stabbed into the ground right in front of her, not a ruler away. She stood there, still as you like, hands on her hips.

Grif froze. Robbie went over. He got a firm grip on the bottom of the handle and pulled it out of the grass. He said something to the mayor, then gathered up the axes and the spade.

The crowd grumbled.

"Je-ed! Je-ed! Je-ed!" Neel clapped his hands.

Lyle joined in.

"Je-ed! Je-ed! Je-ed!"

Everyone joined in.

"Je-ed! Je-ed! Je-ed!"

Lyle and Grif found Jed behind the wall. They pulled him out and lifted him up. He struggled. *Get off*, I heard him shout. But no one listened to him, not tonight.

"Je-ed! Je-ed! Je-ed!"

Robbie and Neel found Lindi and picked her up too.

They lifted the two of them up to the sky. Like offerings.

"Lin-di! Lin-di! Lin-di!"

"Maggie?" Trig shouted over the chanting.

"Yeah?"

"Lin-di! Lin-di! Lin-di!"

"What was wrong with Jed and Lindi, before?" said Trig. "They were being really weird. Didn't you think so, Maggie? Didn't you think so? Why were they being like that? Why did she push me? Why did she say all those things to you?"

"Je-ed! Je-ed! Je-ed!"

"They're just excited," I lied.

I'd never imagined eldests being frightened of anything, least of all going to camp. But Jed and Lindi—they were scared. Really scared.

# Saturday,
# September 6

# Chapter 16

"Here." Jed unstrapped Grandad Cruise's watch from his wrist. "Can't take it with me."

He passed it to me. I held it to my ear.

*Tick. Tick. Tick. Tick. Tick.* Steady as you like.

"I'll look after it," I said. "Till you get back."

Jed did one of his half smiles. "Trig, you can have everything else." He pushed open his bedroom door. "Whatever you want."

He wasn't allowed to take much to camp. Just a few clothes and his billy lamp. That was all.

Trig didn't go in. He started bobbing. He'd be jogging on the spot soon.

"Treat it well, though"—Jed gave Trig a mock punch in the arm—"or you'll be in for it when I get home." He didn't laugh, though. Didn't even smile.

He wasn't coming back. Not to stay. Not for a visit. Not for anything. He wasn't coming back any more than Mom's sister Lil was.

I started bobbing too, just like Trig.

*Got to get out of here. Got to get out.*

I ran downstairs. Out the back door, into the garden. The air was thicker than ever. The neck of my T-shirt was already soaked with sweat. *I hope Elsie was right about the weather.* She said it was going to change. It had to rain. It couldn't carry on like this.

I wrapped Grandad Cruise's watch round my wrist and did it up on the smallest fitting. It was loose, but not so loose it'd fall off. I touched its glassy face.

"Maggie?" Mom stood in the doorway. Mom, who'd been lying to me all this time. Letting me think Jed'd be coming home. "Maggie—are you all ri—"

"Leave me alone."

"Oh, Maggie, I know how you must—"

"You lied about camp."

She frowned. "Lied?"

"Jed's not coming home, is he? Not ever."

Mom's face crumpled. "Maggie—"

"You lied about Aunt Lil."

"We had to, Maggie. It's part of the edict. We have to keep the war quiet. We have to look after the eldests. We have to make sure they—"

"Dad too. Both of you lied—"

"What's going on?"

Trig. He hooked himself under Mom's arm and snugged himself in. "What's Maggie talking about, Mom? What are you talking about, Maggie?"

Mom looked right at me. Her eyes bulged with tears.

*Don't tell Trig.*

*Don't tell Trig.*

"Nothing." I rubbed the old battered watch strap. It was soft between my fingers. "I'm not talking about anything."

I pushed past them back into the house.

"We're just trying to keep you safe, Maggie." Mom hugged Trig into her. "You and Trig."

I thundered up the stairs and dived onto my bed.

Jed was going to fight so I could stay safe.

He wasn't ever coming home.

And the wanderers were out there, keeping their own eldests close.

And what was I doing? Maggie-middler?

Messing about at the boundary with a wanderer girl. Singing songs. Wiggling ears. Stealing food.

I pressed Grandad's watch against my cheek. Cool and smooth.

*If I keep it with me forever, I'll never forget about Jed.*

~ ~ ~

The mayor had her gramophone going in front of her house. She always did when anyone went to camp. Lyle Parker was keeping it steady on its trolley, winding it up when it ran down. It coughed and stuttered and sent scratchy music across the square. Me and Trig covered our ears. Mom and Dad squeezed our shoulders. I shook them off. The whole rest of the town, groggy from the heat and the home brew last night, stood silent around us.

Jed and Lindi came out with the mayor. They each had their billy lamp in one hand and a small bag in the other. The mayor stood herself between them. She gave Lyle a nod. He took the old sock out from under the gramophone and stuffed it into the trumpet, quietening the music.

"What can I say about these brave young eldests?" The mayor's voice carried right across the square. "Nothing, perhaps, that you don't already know, but I've been talking to their parents and their teachers . . ."

The mayor went on. Talked about the time Jed got his head stuck in the railings up at the crescent and old man Parker got him out with carbolic soap. And about how Lindi used to sit on her dad's lap in the tractor pretending to do the steering while he ploughed up the wheat fields.

Jed banged his billy lamp against his leg. Lindi held hers completely still and fixed a smile on her face: closed lips, high cheeks, feet together.

*I don't want to be here. Don't want to watch them get into the mayor's jeep and be driven away.*

Dad squeezed my shoulders again. Mom was right next to him, squeezing Trig's. I wriggled loose.

"These two eldests will be an invaluable asset at camp." Some of Mayor Anderson's hair had fallen out of her ponytail, like bits of old string. "So before they depart for glory, could we all join together in the morning chant?"

The whole town stood straight and proud. Lifted their voices.

*"Our eldests are heroes.*
*Our eldests are special.*
*Our eldests are brave.*

*Shame upon any who holds back an eldest*
*And shame upon their kin.*
*Most of all,*
*Shame upon the wanderers.*

*Let peace settle over the Quiet War,*
*Truly and forever."*

*They really* are *heroes. And special. And brave.*

It felt true and good to say the chant. Truer and gooder than it had ever felt before. It was true and good that I was going to be painting portraits of eldests.

The mayor mouthed something to Neel Parker. He dodged round the side of the house.

After this I'd go straight to the cemetery.

Find Una.

*Shame upon the wanderers.*

I'd carry on with my plan to hand her in. It was the right thing to do. I touched Grandad Cruise's watch, its curved, smooth edges.

*Ter-rutt-terutt-trutt.* The sound of the mayor's jeep, choking into life. It chuggered round the corner into sight, Neel in the driver's seat.

Jed held out his hand to Lindi. She grabbed it, and they climbed in together.

My body lurched forward.

Dad pulled me back.

*Don't go, Jed. Don't go.*

Lyle took the sock out of the trumpet and gave the gramophone a good windup. The music screeched. Trig covered his ears.

Lindi's face—still neat, still bruised—stared from the back window. Mrs. Chowdhry cried out. The crowd wrapped itself around her, hushing her.

Dad's grip hardened on my shoulders.

The music swung round the sides of the square.

Neel got out of the jeep and held the door open for the mayor. She lifted a solemn palm to us and climbed in.

Neel gave the jeep's roof a couple of goodbye smacks. *Thwack, thwack.*

*Churrrrrrr-utt.* Black smoke belched from the back. As they drove off, Jed wrapped an arm round Lindi.

I'm sure he did.

I'm sure.

The crowd murmured and shuffled and loosened.

Mrs. Chowdhry sobbed.

Mom took hold of Trig's hand. "Our eldests are heroes," she said. "Let's go home."

I squirmed out of Dad's grip.

"I'm not coming."

# Chapter 17

I ran.

Faster and faster and faster.

My brother was gone, and he wasn't coming back.

I ran down Frog Alley.

Past the caravans.

Stupid Jed. He drove me mad with his braveness and his specialness and his being an eldest.

Over the ridges.

Across the field.

Faster and faster.

I was going to miss him so much my chest was tearing in two with the whole pain of it.

Up to the cemetery.

Faster and faster.

My brother was gone.

He wasn't coming back.

I had to find out where Una was living. I had to find evidence.

I had to do something. Anything.

I hated wanderers.

*Shame upon the wanderers.*

I hated Una.

*Shame upon Una.*

I collapsed under the tree, on William Whittington. Sweat ran off my hair and behind my ears.

I tried to tighten the strap on Grandad Cruise's watch. My tears dropped onto its round face.

No clanking from Mr. Gebby. The dead relatives were silent too.

Only the crickets were still singing.

I waited.

And waited.

I lay down on William Whittington and cried huge, loud, chest-heaving sobs. Sticky sunshine leaked through the leaves.

I waited two hours, eight minutes, and forty-six seconds.

Grandad Cruise's watch doesn't lie. It's steady as a cart horse.

~ ~ ~

"Hey! Maggie! Maggie!" It was Una, climbing through the hawthorn.

My tears had dried up. My chest had stopped heaving. I was calm.

*Act normal, Maggie. Act normal.*

"You okay?" she said. "You been crying? You have, you've been crying. What's wrong, Maggie? What is it?"

"Nothing," I said. "I'm fine."

"No, you're not. I can tell, Maggie. What's wrong?"

"It's nothing." But the tears brimmed up in my eyes again. "You wouldn't understand."

"Oh no? Try me." She sat her dirty, deceitful wanderer self right down next to me.

"My brother's gone away. That's all." A tear escaped from the inside corner of my eye and rolled down the side of my nose. "You haven't got a brother. You wouldn't understand." I edged away from her, so our legs wouldn't touch. I plucked at the overgrown grass so I didn't have to look at her.

"I *did* have a brother, so I do understand. Kind of, anyway."

I stopped picking at the grass. I looked up. "You had a brother?"

"Yes. He went to camp. Is that where your brother's gone? Do they still have camp? I was only a baby when mine went, so I don't miss him. Well, not like you're missing yours."

She had a brother who went to camp?

"What?" I said. "How?"

"Felix, his name was. He was much older than me. But you don't want to hear about all that when you're feeling so bad, Maggie."

*She must be lying.*

*Wanderers don't send their eldests to camp.*

"Tell you what," she said. "Come through the boundary again, properly this time. Come and meet my dad. It won't bring your brother back, but we've got a Cleercan to filter water and a fire hole to heat it up. I dug a really good one this time, it hardly makes any smoke at all. I can make you a cup of tea. And tea's good, when you're feeling bad. Especially tea made like Grandad taught me. Come on, Maggie, I'll get you back to your hawthorn hedge before anyone even notices you're gone."

Felix.

Camp.

Lies.

My head was heavy and tired and full of tears.

*But I should go. Find out where she lives. Get some evidence.*

I pulled up the bottom of my T-shirt and rubbed my eyes dry. Swallowed down the crying.

"All right, then." I made my face into a smile. "A cup of tea would be great."

# Chapter 18

The hawthorn scratched at me from the outside, my heart thumped at me from the inside.

I ignored them both.

I pushed the whole way through.

Maggie Cruise—boundary breaker.

I stood up on the other side.

Brighter, fresher grass. The smell of crisp, red apples.

My knees jittered.

"I . . . um . . . I . . ." Words floundered around in my mouth.

No one ever went outside the town. No one except the mayor. And the eldests, of course, on their way to camp.

*It puts the whole of Fennis Wick in danger.*

This was a bad idea.

"I think maybe I should just go home." I stepped backward.

*There must be another way to catch a wanderer.*

"You can't!" said Una. "You've done the hardest bit. Come on, it's this way."

She turned toward the forest, looked back at me, and lifted her elbow out to the side.

Did she want me to link my arm through hers?

Like friends?

No one had ever wanted to link arms with me before. Not ever.

"C'mon." She wiggled her elbow.

I slipped my arm through.

Her skin was warm with dirt and sunshine. She smelled of trees and unwashed hair.

I glanced behind me, back toward Fennis Wick.

*No one's seen me. No one knows.*

I walked beside her, through the brighter, fresher grass.

Maybe Una wasn't like other wanderers.

I mean, she couldn't have killed Mr. Wetheral's family. She was too young. And she wouldn't have anyway. She just wouldn't have.

Maybe she wasn't dangerous or deceitful at all. And being dirty, well, that wasn't such a bad thing, was it?

And if she'd lost her mom, *and* her grandad *and* her brother, well, that was terrible. Really terrible.

"Did you really have a brother who went to camp?" I said.

"Course," she said. "Did you think I was lying? I'd never lie to you, Maggie. We're best friends, aren't we?"

*Best friends.*

I'd never had a best friend. Not in my whole life.

She grinned her gappy grin. The long grass brushed against my legs.

She squeezed my arm in hers.

*Best friends.*

I touched the front of Grandad Cruise's watch.

~ ~ ~

The forest started off as just a few trees dotted around us, but it soon got thicker and we had to let go arms. Una trotted doe-like between branches, ferns, and moss, even in her rain boots. I stumbled after her, trying to tread in her footsteps. There wasn't any path.

"How do you remember the way?" I said.

"S'easy. I follow the marks. Look here, on this tree." She pointed to some chalk marks on a tree trunk. Three slanted lines. I'd never have seen them if she hadn't shown me.

"This means carry on in that direction, see? Like this?" She held her hand underneath them, slanting upwards, palm face-down, just like the lines. "So that way's home."

"Did you make them—the marks?"

"These ones, yeah."

We carried on through the trees and the thickening under-growth. A robin sang a high trill above our heads, but closer to the ground brambles clawed my calves. I stopped to wipe off some blood. At least it was cooler here under the branches.

Every time Una followed a chalk sign, she pointed it out to me. "Look. Here's some signs left by other wanderers."

Three lines again, but the bottom one was wiggly.

"That means there's a water supply nearby. And this"—she pointed at a rectangle underneath the lines—"means there's shelter. It's how we found a place to stay."

"Are they always there, those signs?"

"Not always. The chalk washes off after two or three rainfalls."

I staggered on through the brambles and bracken.

"Look—we're here." Una pointed through the trees.

And there it was, a small barn, snugged into a clearing.

~ ~ ~

The barn only had two walls. The other sides were open, with supporting posts keeping the roof up.

"Dad! Dad!" Una ran in and swung round a post. "I've brought someone to meet you. It's Maggie. Maggie who gave us the food and the antibiotics."

I hung back outside. There were tree stumps dotted around, looked like they'd been used for tables or workbenches. They had stuff on top of them—leather pouches, a wooden spoon, a few cups and bowls, some books. Three billy lamps sat out on one, soaking up the sunshine.

Inside the barn, bright-colored sacks were hooked along the walls—green and blue and yellow. A bundle of blankets was heaped in one corner.

Una grabbed a plastic water carrier. "We're going to fill up the Cleercan, Dad."

Who was she talking to? The place was empty.

"C'mon, Maggie," she said.

"Mmmm?" The bundle of blankets shifted and a groany, grimy face emerged.

Mr. Opal.

"We're going to the brook," said Una. "To fill up the Cleercan."

"What's going on?" He was a big mass of rust-colored hair. If Mom was here she'd have whipped the scissors out before you could say *haircut*.

"Maggie's here. My friend. I told you about her. She gave us the food and the medicine."

He bolted upright. Pulled a pair of glasses from his tangled hair and put them on. He glared at me.

"Didn't I tell you never to bring anyone here, Una?"

"She's just come for some tea. Her brother's gone away. I thought it'd—"

"Get out of here!" Mr. Opal lurched toward me, pulling his blankets with him.

I stumbled backward into a tree stump.

"Dad, don't! Your leg!"

He fell back down, wincing, gripping his thigh, but he kept his eyes fixed on me.

*I shouldn't have come*. This was a real wanderer. Dirty and dangerous. Mayor Anderson was right. Of course she was.

"Mr. Opal, I'm sorry, I—"

"This is an unknown town, Una. Didn't you listen to me? You have to assume it's unfriendly." He got up again, half standing, half crouching. He held his leg and grimaced.

"But she's all right, Dad. It's Maggie—she's my friend, *our* friend. She helped us."

He felt around on the floor beside him, picked up a pitchfork and pointed it at me. "Get out of here."

*I shouldn't have come.*

*I'm not a hero.*

*I'm not an eldest.*

*I'm not brave.*

My mouth dried up.

Mr. Opal—Una's dad—he could've killed Mr. Wetheral's family. He really could've.

I've put the whole of Fennis Wick at risk. Mom, Dad, Trig—everyone.

"You can't trust them, Una." He hopped toward me, blanket fixed round him with one hand and pitchfork held fast in the other. He growled with the pain.

*Stay calm, Maggie.*

*You can outrun him.*

"I had to trust someone, Dad. You were really sick. We had nothing to eat. She saved your life. She saved both our lives."

"Argh." He tripped over the blanket, fell to the ground, eyes squeezed shut. He clutched his leg. "What have you done, Una? You shouldn't have brought her here."

I grabbed something from the nearest tree stump. Something covered in leather.

Evidence.

I shoved it into the front of my shorts and pulled my T-shirt over the top.

"But, Dad, she's my friend. She won't tell anyone about us. I know it. You won't, will you, Maggie?"

There were tears in Una's eyes. Real tears.

I took a step backward.

And another.

"You won't, will you, Maggie?"

I turned and ran.

# Chapter 19

I scrambled up the stairs and collapsed onto my bed.

"Maggie?" Dad called up after me. "Is that you? We've been worried about you."

"I'm fine," I shouted back. "I'm fine."

*I'm not fine.*

*I'm not.*

My ribs heaved. *Up-down-up-down-up-down.*

I pulled the leather thing from my shorts, turned it round in my hands.

A sheath.

One end was flapped over and tied up with a lace.

I untied it, unfolded it. Pulled out a knife.

It was well used. Dented, dulled, dirty. But sharp.

Its wooden handle had a design carved into it. I tilted it toward the light. Fine antennae, wide wings, whorled patterns. Butterflies. I ran my fingers over it. The carvings dipped and curled under my fingertips.

Now I had proof.

I'd take it to the mayor. Soon as she was back from camp.

She'd know what to do.

"Maggie?"

I shoved the knife under my pillow. Fumbled with the sheath.

"Come down, love. I've got some food out." Dad opened the door, just a little. "Leftovers. Thought we could all eat together. The four of us, I mean."

"Yeah," I said. "Okay."

The four of us.

Not five anymore.

Una's dad had never sent anyone to camp. He'd lied to her. She'd believed him, but there never was an older brother, was there?

*Deceitful.*

*And now I've gone and done it, haven't I? Gone out of the boundary. Made contact with a dirty, dangerous wanderer. Maybe he'll come after me. Or worse, maybe he'll come after Mom or Dad or Trig.*

*Stupid, stupid Maggie-middler.*

*Mayor Anderson'll know what to do. She'll keep us safe.*

~ ~ ~

We sat in the kitchen. Me, Trig, Mom, Dad, and a huge gaping space where Jed should've been.

"Aren't you going to eat anything?" said Dad.

I stared at the cold meat, the tomato pastries, the goldie pie. My empty stomach pushed up at my throat. "I'm not hungry, Dad."

"Me neither," said Trig.

"Me neither," said Mom.

Six o'clock in the evening. I left the house, the sheathed knife tucked into my shorts again. It pushed into my stomach with every step.

"Hello, Maggie." It was Mr. Gebby, heading home.

I didn't answer. Kept my eyes on the ground. One foot in front of the other. Guilty step after guilty step after guilty step. The whole town at risk. Even Mr. Gebby.

It should've been getting cooler this time of day, but it was only getting hotter. Mr. Wetheral's cat was spread out in the shade, just at the end of Frog Alley. A frog hopped past, safe in the heat.

Even the pigeons were lazy from the sun. They waddled off as I walked through the square, only one bothering to flap up onto Andrew Solsbury's foot.

The mayor's house towered over me. I knocked on the door.

No answer.

I sat down on the step and waited.

Huge bruised clouds hung low, blocking the sun. Blankety air wrapped itself round me. My sweaty knees slid against each other and my T-shirt was damp under my arms.

Elsie was right. There was another storm coming and it was coming soon. Everything was going to change.

# Chapter 20

The air grew even darker as Mayor Anderson's jeep juddered into the square. A wind gusted in, whipping about the statue, scattering leaves. The skin on my arms gave a shiver, first time in months.

The jeep was piled up with boxes on the roof rack. But there was no Jed in the back seat anymore. And no Lindi. They were gone. Properly gone.

The mayor peered at me and turned in beside the house. I followed round.

She got out, slammed the door, and opened up the back. She had a green-and-black plaid shirt on, different from the one she'd been wearing earlier. The wind caught her hair and threw it across her face. She pulled the straggles away from her mouth. "All right, Maggie?"

Neel came out from the back of the house. "Good trip, Mayor Anderson? Get all the way to the city today?" He undid the straps on the roof rack, freeing up the boxes.

"No." She glanced at me. "Just camp today. Up to the city

next week. Maggie? You all right? Your brother went off okay, if that's what you want to know."

"Er, that's good," I said, "but I . . . um . . . I—"

"Speak up. I haven't got all day." She rubbed her arms and looked at the sky. "Cold wind." She leaned into the jeep. Pointed out some crates to Neel.

*She's right. Speak up, Maggie. Speak up.*

"I . . . um . . . found some wanderers, Mayor Anderson. I found them, and I, well—I think I've put the whole town at risk."

She looked at me. "You're telling me a little middler girl found some wanderers?"

Neel and the mayor smirked at each other. He hitched a crate out of the trunk and took it round the back of the house.

Mayor Anderson lifted her chin. "Where did you find these wanderers, then? You haven't been out of boundary, have you, Miss Cruise?"

"No! No. I met them in the . . . um . . . cemetery. There's a girl. Her name's Una and—"

"Look," she said, "I know what it's like being a middler. I was one myself. Always making stuff up to get attention."

Mayor Anderson? A middler? She must be, now I thought about it. If she's here instead of camp.

"So if this is all make-believe, can we stop right now?" She pulled a crate across the back of the jeep. "It's going to rain any moment and I need to get these inside." She took something out of the crate. Bananas. Real bananas. Five or six, bunched together. Like claws. She sniffed at them, and put them back.

"I'm not making it up, Mayor Anderson. It's true. This wanderer, Una, she came to find some food and now I'm worried because—"

"You're in the way, Maggie." The mayor pushed me to one side so Neel could get past.

*Flash.*

Lightning. Elsie's storm. It lit up the mayor's face for a split second. Her yellow teeth. Her spidery skin.

"You have to do something," I said. "I met her dad—he's dirty, and dangerous, and deceitful. I think the town's in danger."

A rumble of thunder rolled across the sky.

The wind flung Mayor Anderson's hair forward again. She pushed it out of her eyes. "Look, Maggie, I really don't have—"

"I can prove I met them," I said. "Look."

I took the sheath out from my shorts. Unwrapped the knife.

*Flash.*

"It's got butterflies on the handle." I held it up. "It's not from Fennis Wick. I took it from Una's dad. He's a wanderer, a real one."

She looked at the knife.

A second clap of thunder barrelled above us. A thick drop of rain hit the blade. I wiped it off.

"Where did you get that?" she said.

Another raindrop. I wiped it again.

"From the wanderer, like I said. What if he comes—Mr. Opal—what if he comes and starts setting fire to our houses?"

Another drop. And another. And another. Splashing off the metal.

She took the knife. Ran her fingers over the butterflies, just like I'd done. The rain fell harder and harder, onto our heads, onto her fingers, onto the blade.

She stared at the knife. Turned it round.

"I've never seen anything like this in Fennis Wick," she said.

"That's because it's not from Fennis Wick. I got it from the wanderers, like I told you."

The rain bolted down.

The mayor turned a quarter step so Neel couldn't see the knife. He carried on unloading the crates as if it wasn't even raining at all.

"You reckon you can show me where these wanderers are?" she said.

"Yes!" She believed me. "I can, I really can." Rain ran into my eyes. "But the girl, Una, she's not like normal wanderers. She's good. You can leave her alone. It's her dad that's dirty and dangerous and deceitful, so you should really just be—"

"Quiet, Cruise." She held a finger up in front of my face. "Listen to me."

"But—"

"*Listen. To. Me.*" She looked me right in the eye, rain pelting between us. "This is how it's going to be. You help me find this pair and I'll not tell anyone you've been associating with the enemy. All right?"

My throat went tight.

"All right, Cruise?"

"Yes. Okay. Yes, Mayor Anderson."

She slid the knife into its sheath and tucked it into her back pocket. Her hair clung to her neck in wet clumps. "Right now I want you to gather up the other Parker boys for me. All three of them, if you can find them. Tell 'em the mayor requires their assistance."

Lightning flashed again.

I raced across the square, crashing through the puddles and the pummeling rain.

"Robbie! Grif! Lyle!"

A third bellow of thunder galloped after me.

# Chapter 21

The rain was gone. The cemetery was damp and dripping.

Grif looked at the thinnest part of the hawthorn. He gave a long, low whistle. "Came in through there, did they? Well, I never."

Lyle stuck his hands in his pockets and kicked at the hedge, spraying rainwater over Grif and Robbie.

"Oi! Watch out!"

"What's the fuss? We're already as wet as we can possibly get. Bit more's not going to make any difference."

"So, you want us to go through, Mayor Anderson?" Robbie rubbed his top lip.

"That's exactly what I want. Which way did you say it was, Maggie?"

I pulled back some of the wet, spiky branches. Pointed toward the trees.

"Over there," I said. "In the forest."

"And there're signs, you say?"

"Uh-huh. Chalk signs, Una told me. If the rain hasn't washed them off. Three lines like this"—I held up my hand—"means you have to go that way. There's one with wiggly lines when you're nearby. That means water. And there's one with a rectangle underneath too. That means shelter."

"Did you get that, boys? We're looking for chalk signs." The mayor ran her tongue along the front of her teeth. "You've done well, Maggie. Now, you get off home."

I picked at the skin on my thumb.

What was Una doing, right now, in the barn?

Was she filling up the Cleercan? Making a fire?

She wasn't expecting the Parker brothers, that's for sure.

"Did you hear what I said, Maggie? You can go now."

"You'll leave Una alone, though?" I said. "She hasn't done anything wrong. She's a good wanderer. It's just her dad who's dangerous."

Grif sniggered. "A good wanderer," he said, elbowing Lyle in the arm.

"Go home," said the mayor. "Leave the rest to us. Come on, boys, let's get through this hedge."

I stepped back a few paces. The air was lighter after the rain. Easier to breathe. But it didn't feel as good as I thought it would.

The mayor and the Parker brothers crashed through the hedge. Made the thin part even thinner, so I could see through it even from back here. They marched toward the forest, stamping down the brighter, fresher grass.

I ran my fingers over Grandad Cruise's watch.

I'd done the right thing. Completely the right thing. The mayor was protecting Fennis Wick. Wanderers were bad, apart from Una. And they were going to leave Una alone.

There was a tiny wind-up knob on the side of the watch. It had little ridges all round the edge. I ran my fingernail over them.

Jed. What was he doing now? His first evening at camp.

*Hope he's still with Lindi.*

I walked under Lindi's tree, between William Whittington and Georgina Millicent Cruise.

The dead relatives were silent. Not a word. Not a whisper.

Maybe chalk marks didn't really last very long. Maybe they couldn't have survived a downpour like that.

# Sunday,
# September 7

# Chapter 22

Sunday. Una's made-up birthday.

I pulled up the blackout shade. A dull, gray sky. The first in ages. Thin rain pattered the window. Goosebumps shivered up my arms. Autumn.

I told Una I'd go to the cemetery. Do the things you do when it's your birthday.

I stood in front of the mirror. Tried to wiggle my ears. Hopeless.

An ache dug at my chest. Una would know it was me who turned her dad in. Would she even want to see me anymore?

I picked up my shorts.

Too cold today.

I pulled on a pair of long pants and a sweater instead.

~ ~ ~

I sat on William Whittington, a big slice of Dad's elderflower drizzle in a bag beside me—birthday cake. I had a banana too. The mayor dropped some off early this morning, while I was still in bed. Mom showed me how to peel them.

Wind swept through the branches of the trees, shook the leaves. Old, dead relatives whispering.

Were they whispering about me?

The thin rain kept on falling. It seeped into my coat, then my sweater. It soaked the bag and turned the cake into damp elderflower mush.

I shivered in the September air.

Una didn't come.

# Monday,
# September 8

# Chapter 23

*"Good morning, Mrs. Zimmerman;*
*Good morning, Mr. Temple;*
*Good morning, Miss Conteh;*
*Good morning, Mr. Webster;*
*Good morning, EVERYONE."*

"It's weird, isn't it? Being here without Jed and Lindi. Isn't it, Maggie? It's weird." Trig spoke so close to my ear his lips actually slobbered on me. Yuck. I pushed him away.

"Heads down, please, for the morning chant." Mrs. Zimmerman clasped her hands and tilted her head.

I squeezed my eyes tight shut. Focused on the words.

*"Our eldests are heroes.*
*Our eldests are special.*
*Our eldests are brave.*

*Shame upon any who holds back an eldest*
*And shame upon their kin.*

*Most of all,*
*Shame upon the wanderers.*

*Let peace settle over the Quiet War,*
*Truly and forever."*


"I have a very special announcement to make this morning." Mrs. Zimmerman's cheekbones tightened into a smile. "I have been informed by Mayor Anderson herself that one of our pupils has performed an exemplary service to our community."

I looked up.

"This Class Four pupil skillfully spotted evidence of wanderers near the town boundary and reported it to the mayor. In doing so she has protected our town—and our families—from a distinct and likely danger."

Me. Mrs. Zimmerman was talking about me. The whole school was gazing up, listening. No fidgeting. No yawning.

"Mayor Anderson sent out a party to investigate. A wanderer girl of fourteen was rescued from the settlement and her wanderer father was dealt with."

Fourteen?

Did she mean Una?

"The wanderer girl is being well cared for in the mayor's house and will be taken to camp as soon as possible."

Camp?

Una? Going to camp?

"So, thanks to one of our very own pupils—a middler, in fact—this wanderer will have the glorious opportunity to serve her country, and our town is safe once more." Mrs. Zimmerman smiled again. "Our Class Four pupil has helped not only her community but also her whole country. She's a very special girl—a very special middler."

*Please don't say my name.*

*Please don't say it.*

"So I'd like her to stand up for a round of applause."

*No, please, no, no.*

"Maggie Cruise? I can see you there, hiding next to your brother! Come on, stand up."

Trig stared at me with his O-shaped mouth.

"Stand up, Maggie! Stand up!"

Hands shoved at me.

"Stand up! Stand up!"

My head swirled. I pressed my hands onto Mr. Webster's smooth wooden floor and wobbled to a stand.

They all clapped for me.

A sea of faces looking up, cheering for Maggie-middler.

It was exactly what I'd dreamed of.

I was special.

I was a hero.

A lonely, miserable hero. Who'd lost the best friend she'd ever had.

I buried my face in my hands.

~ ~ ~

After school I ran home to get changed. Didn't even wait for Trig. Then I went straight to the mayor's.

*KNOCK-KNOCK-KNOCK-KNOCK-KNOCK.*

No answer.

*KNOCK-KNOCK-KNOCK-KNOCK-KNOCK.*

*Una must be in there. Mrs. Zimmerman said she was.* I had to speak to her.

*KNOCK-KNOCK-KNOCK-KNOCK-KNOCK.*

No answer.

I walked backward into the square, looked up at the windows. Was that a movement—a shadow—a someone? In the very top window?

The highest window in town.

"Una? Una!" I shouted up. "Una!"

No.

Nothing.

No one.

I walked to the middle of the square. Sat on Andrew Solsbury's pigeon-dirtied feet.

If Una was fourteen, it was right that she should go to camp. Of course it was. Her dad had lied to her about having a brother. Una was an eldest, and eldests had to go to camp.

It was right.

And good.

And glorious.

But I wanted to see her, I had to see her, just one last time before she went.

And what about her dad, Mr. Opal? He'd been *dealt with*.

My stomach curdled.

*Dealt with.* What did that mean? What if they'd hurt him?

They wouldn't have hurt him. They wouldn't.

But what if they had? Una would never forgive me. Not ever. Even if he'd lied to her. Even if he was dirty and dangerous and deceitful.

I got up. Walked out of the square, down Frog Alley, straight past Elsie in her vegetable patch.

"Need a forecast, Cruise girl? Nature doesn't lie."

I kept walking.

~ ~ ~

The barn was ruined. Sacks ripped off the walls; cups and bowls smashed and scattered. Clothes and blankets strewn between trees. Pulpy, torn sheets of paper flapped and draped through the bracken. The billy lamps lay broken on their sides and the Cleercan was squashed, like someone had jumped on it.

Everything ruined.

*Did the Parkers do all this?*

I picked up a piece of cloth. A girl's top. *Must be Una's.* I folded it carefully. Placed it on one of the tree stumps. Then I gathered up some of the paper. It was printed, torn from a book. There were so many sheets, all over the place. I couldn't get them all.

I lifted a blanket. Some things rolled out onto the ground— Mr. Opal's glasses and a small brown bottle. The trellicillin. There was still some left. I put it in my pocket. The glasses were in two pieces—one arm broken off. Where was Mr. Opal? How was he going to see without them? I tried to fix them back together but the hinge had snapped.

Maybe it didn't matter. Maybe he didn't need them anymore. Not if he was—

"Urrrrrrrrr."

I froze.

"Urrrrrrrr."

Was someone there? Behind the barn?

I scanned the ground—there had to be something here I could protect myself with.

"Urrrrrrrrr."

I grabbed a saucepan. Held it high with shaking hands. Edged round the barn wall.

Nothing.

"Urrrrrrrrr."

The trees.

It was coming from the trees.

I crept forward, saucepan high.

Something moved in the wet bracken.

I stepped closer.

A face. Bleeding, battered, bruised.

"Who is it? Who's there?" His voice was weak.

"It's me, Mr. Opal. It's Maggie."

# Chapter 24

*Should I move him? Leave him there?*

*I wish Trig was here. Trig'd know what to do. He's good at all that first-aid kind of stuff.*

"W-water," he rasped.

Water. Of course.

I ran back to the barn. There was still a bit in the bottom of the squashed Cleercan. I found a cup on the floor, poured it in.

I held it to his mouth as he sipped.

It brought some life back to him. He grabbed my wrist. Hard. The cup fell from my hand. The rest of the water sank into the ground.

"Una," he said. "Where's Una?"

"She's in town. At the mayor's house."

"She's alive?"

"Yes, yes, she's alive."

He let go, collapsed down onto the forest floor. I rubbed my wrist where he'd gripped it.

Mr. Opal patted his hand around on the top of his head.

"Are you looking for your glasses? They're in the barn. Hold on."

I fetched the glasses. Handed him the two pieces.

"I tried to fix them, Mr. Opal, but—"

"You stupid girl." He held them to his bleeding face. "You stupid, stupid girl. You told them about us."

He tried to get up but fell back down again. His glasses tumbled off.

I picked them up.

*What should I do?* I couldn't leave him under the trees.

"Mr. Opal," I said, "it's wet out here. I think we should get you inside."

He let me help him. We made our way to the barn, me half dragging and him half crawling.

I sat him against the back wall. He panted and wheezed and coughed and cried with all the pain. I searched the sacks that had been torn from the walls, found a dry blanket and wrapped it round him.

"Here." I took the trellicillin out. "You should take one of these."

I gave him a tablet and emptied the last drops of water from the Cleercan into the cup.

He swallowed it down. Rested his head back against the wall.

"I should've taught her better," he said. "Should've made sure she didn't trust people who can't be trusted."

Me. He was talking about me.

"Mr. Opal, I told Mayor Anderson to leave Una alone. I told

her she was a good person. I told her she wasn't like other wanderers. I told her she should just go after . . ."

*Shut up, Maggie. Just shut up.*

"Just go after me?" He coughed. His face crunched up.

"You're a wanderer," I said. "You selfishly keep your own eldests close. You're dangerous. And deceitful."

"Is that you speaking, Maggie? Or is that your Mayor Anderson?"

I stood tall. "My brother's gone to camp."

"Camp?"

"I couldn't be more proud," I said. "He's protecting us, protecting you. And I don't want Una to go to camp any more than you do. She's the best friend I ever had, but it's right that she goes, just like it's right that my brother's gone. We all have to send our eldests, even—"

"What? What do you mean—Una going to camp?"

"The mayor's taking her. And . . ." I took a breath. I had to say it. "Shame on you for not sending her before. Shame on you."

"But there's no such thing as camp." Mr. Opal squinted up at me. "Not anymore."

*"Shame upon any who holds back an eldest."*

"Oh, just stop with your parroting." Mr. Opal's voice echoed off the barn walls and out into the forest. "Camp finished years ago. Where is your mayor taking my daughter?"

Deceitful.

Dangerous.

He patted the floor around him. "Where are my glasses? What in hell did you do with my glasses?"

I passed them over.

He held them up to his face and looked at me properly. "Now, you listen to me. I'm very sorry that your brother has gone wherever he's gone, but you cannot let them take my daughter. You cannot let them do it."

*"Each one of them will fight for country and gl—"*

"I told you, there is no camp!" His voice got even louder.

"You're a liar!" I covered my ears, tried to make my voice as big as his.

"Look, look, I'm sorry, all right?" He held a calming hand forward, softened his voice. "But camp doesn't—" He fumbled with his glasses. "What I mean is . . . I've already sent my eldest to camp."

"I don't believe you."

"Una's older brother went to camp, years ago. She's not an eldest, so even if there was still a camp, she doesn't belong there."

"She never had a brother. You lied to her and you're lying to me."

He gave up with his glasses and leaned back against the wall. "You ignorant girl." He rested his arms across his stomach, one half of his broken glasses in each hand. They lifted and lowered with his raspy, painful breaths. "You stupid, stupid girl."

"You're lying," I said, but I whispered it this time.

Dirty.

Dangerous.

Deceitful.

He took an extra deep breath and sat back upright. "Make yourself useful," he said. "There's some tape in one of those sacks. The green one. See it?"

I found the sack, got the tape out.

"Stick this arm back onto my glasses. It's the least you can do."

I took the glasses, stuck them back together. There was a messy clump of tape at one side, but they stayed on his face without him holding them.

"Now, that book." He pointed to the curled, soggy pages, still all over the place. "Find me the cover."

"The cover?"

"Now, Maggie. Right now. You say you're Una's friend? Well, I'm going to prove to you she shouldn't be at *camp*—or wherever she's going—and if you're really her friend, you'll listen. Find. Me. The. Cover."

I searched inside half-emptied sacks, between broken cups, under torn clothing.

I found it behind the barn. A stiff book cover, lying open in the damp. *The New Poets.* Didn't look new. Looked ancient. I wiped it against my pants.

"Good. Now, I need my knife," said Mr. Opal. He pulled himself across the barn floor, searching for his knife.

He wasn't going to find it.

"Does it have butterflies carved into the handle?"

"Mmm?"

"Your knife. Has it got butterflies on the handle?"

"Yes. You seen it?"

"I took it. Saturday, when I was here. The mayor's got it now. I'm sorry."

He sniffed. Scratched the side of his face. Winced.

"You really did us over, didn't you, Maggie? Good and proper. That green sack again—you got it? Should be a penknife in the inside pocket. If you didn't give that one to your mayor as well."

The penknife was still there. I passed it to him and he pulled it open. He set the book cover across his knees.

There was tape—like I'd fixed the glasses with—all round the edges on the inside of the cover. He used the knife to score along three sides, then picked at one corner. He peeled back a layer of paper and eased something out.

A photograph.

A boy's face grinned out from the shiny surface. Big gap between his two front teeth. Hair the exact same yellow as pound-cake mixture, right before you bake it.

Mr. Opal held the photo by its very edges with his muddy, bloody hands.

"Felix," he said, his face wet with tears. "My boy, Felix. Went to camp. Real camp. Thirteen years ago."

# Chapter 25

"I don't understand." It was lies, wasn't it? All that stuff about Una having a brother?

But the face on the photograph grinned out at me with its gappy smile. It was so much like her.

"It's not hard." Mr. Opal wiped his face. "I had a son, he went to camp. Una was born a few months before he left. She never really knew him."

"But wanderers don't send their eldests to camp. Mayor Anderson says so."

"You've got to stop believing everything this Mayor Anderson tells you, Maggie. Got to start thinking for yourself." He tapped hard on his head with his dirty fingers. "Some wanderers sent their eldests to camp, some didn't."

"*Sent?* What do you mean, *sent?*" I said.

"The point is, it was all about freedom. Freedom to make the choice you want to make. Not having some self-important mayor telling you what you can and can't do all the time. D'you see?"

No. Not really.

"But what did you mean when you said *sent?*"

"Mmmm?" Mr. Opal gazed at the photograph.

"*Some wanderers sent their eldests.* That's what you said. So they don't send them now? So Mayor Anderson's right?"

He pushed his glasses onto his head. Rubbed his eyes. "What does she tell you, this Mayor Anderson of yours? Does she tell you your brother's off to fight the glorious fight in the Quiet War? To keep you all safe back home?"

"Of course. He's a hero. They all are."

He balanced his glasses back on his nose. They dipped down on the taped side.

"They're heroes all right, I'll give you that. And until a few years back that's exactly what they were doing. Keeping us all safe, fighting in the Quiet War."

"The eldest edict," I said.

"Exactly. Good old Andrew Solsbury. Took all the eldests off to war. Saved the country when it needed saving the most. Statue of him in every town. Brought us all peace and happiness, as long as you didn't have the misfortune to be born first. Couldn't afford hospitals for them, or a postal system, or transport back home. Just sent them off and that was that. Gone."

"But it's good and brave," I said. "And right."

"Maybe, for a while." He placed the photograph down on top of the book cover. "Pass me that Cleercan, will you? I'll see if I can knock it back into shape."

"What d'you mean, *for a while?*"

He sighed. "I should never have come so close to this town," he said to himself.

"Tell me, Mr. Opal. What d'you mean?" I picked up the Cleercan, handed it over.

He pressed it from both sides.

"It's what I've been trying to tell you, Maggie. There is no camp anymore. War's over. Finished years ago."

War's over? What was he talking about?

He twisted the can round, pressed it again. "But I can hazard a guess at what your mayor's game is. Came across it once before, in a different town. Half deserted and miles from anywhere, just like this one. Handful of corrupt officials who just can't give up on the eldest edict. They get too much from it, see? And the rest of the country's too busy trying to keep itself alive to take any real notice."

*Pop.* The Cleercan clicked back into shape.

He was lying. This was just another dirty lie from a deceitful wanderer.

"That's not true," I said. "We chant for peace in every school assembly. Why would we do that, if the war was over? And we pull the blackout shades down every night—because of the war. And why would we send our eldests away, if they didn't need to go?"

He handed the Cleercan to me. "Would you fill it up? Brook's just over there." He pointed through the trees.

"You're talking garbage," I said.

He fixed me in the eye. "Now, listen to me, Maggie. Your

mayor. Does she ever bring things back from wherever she goes? Things for the town? Nice things for herself? For her friends? For you, even?"

Gas.

Bananas.

Lyle's dark glasses.

"Sometimes," I said.

"You bet she does. If she keeps the eldests coming, she can trade them in. Maybe up at the city, maybe through a middleman. Then they get traded on as labor, overseas maybe. Mayor gets hold of goods she'd never be able to lay her hands on otherwise. And she kids herself it's okay to be selling fourteen-year-olds because she's supplying her town with oil and gas and imported food and new clothes."

"I don't believe you. You're lying. Mayor Anderson would never do anything like that. She looks after us. You're a dirty, deceitful wanderer. I bet you even set fire to Mr. Wetheral's house too, didn't you? I bet it was you."

Mr. Opal grabbed my wrist again. "I don't know what you're talking about. I don't even know who Mr. Wetheral is. But that's okay. You can believe what you want about the war and you can believe what you want about me. I don't care." His grip tightened. "Look, all I want—all I've ever wanted—is to stay away from this madness and to keep my family safe. Una's the only one left now. She's all I've got. And even if the war was still going, she's not an eldest. This is the evidence right here."

He stabbed his finger at the photograph. "It's an official eldest photo. Look, there, in the corner. That's proof my boy went to camp."

There was some tiny writing, right near the edge.

"I can't read that," I said. "It could say anything."

"It doesn't, though. It's proof that Felix went to camp. I need you to take this photo and show it to your misguided town and get Una released. She's all I've got. I'd go myself, but I can't move ten feet with this leg. I'm relying on you, Maggie. You got her caught up in this—you've got to sort it out."

He held out the photograph.

"Take it," he said. "If you're really her friend, you'll take it and you'll bring her back to me. Take it, Maggie. Please."

He squeezed my wrist so hard I tumbled over.

He let go. "I'm sorry," he said. "I didn't mean to . . ."

I got up again. "S'all right. I'll go and fill this."

I took the Cleercan through the trees and found the fast, rippling brook. I dunked the can in and filled it up. The water ran clear and cold round my fingers.

It was all lies. What he said about the war being over. It had to be lies. There was no way Mayor Anderson would trade in our eldests. But maybe Una really did have a brother. And if she did—if she wasn't an eldest—she shouldn't be going to camp.

I went back and put the can down beside Mr. Opal. Then I picked up the photograph and slipped it back under the cover of *The New Poets*. It'd keep it safe while I was carrying it.

Mr. Opal shivered. His face was a big old mess of tears and dirt and blood and beard.

"Una said you had a fire hole," I said. "Shall I light it, before I go?"

"No, I'll do it myself. You have to hurry. You have to get there before it's too late."

# Chapter 26

*Peck-peck-peck.*

The woodpecker pecked at Mr. Wetheral's door.

*Peck-peck-peck.*

*Peck-peck-peck.*

Come on. Come on.

The door opened. The Siamese cat shot out.

"Maggie." Mr. Wetheral smiled his lopsided smile. "How delightful to see you. Are you okay? You look rather upset."

"Mr. Wetheral, I need your help. There's no one else I can ask." I glanced behind me.

"Are you afraid of something, Maggie?"

I was. I was afraid.

Stupid Maggie-middler. Afraid of everything.

He opened the door wider and stepped to one side.

"Perhaps we'd better talk inside."

~ ~ ~

"Mother? Maggie's here. Would you bring us some tea?"

I followed Mr. Wetheral into the back room.

"Sorry about the mess," he said. "I'd like to be able to say it's not always like this, but it wouldn't be true. I like to have my things around me."

"It's okay, Mr. Wetheral, I don't mind."

I picked my way across the room, shoved a pile of books to the back of an armchair and perched on the front. Mr. Wetheral took some mugs from the coffee table, squeezed them onto the edge of the mantelpiece and sat in their place.

"So," he said, "my guess is you've come to talk to me about the wanderers. You've been helping them, this last week. Taking them food. You've even been out there, haven't you? Beyond the hawthorn?"

If I was Trig, my mouth would've done an O.

He scratched his gloved hand.

"Would you mind if I removed my glove? It gets so itchy underneath."

"I don't mind at all."

He pulled the glove off and blew on the back of his hand. The skin was tight, creased, fragile.

"How did you know?" I said.

He scrunched his fingers into a fist, then splayed them out wide. "Mother saw you first, up at the boundary, oh, a week ago now. And then I saw you too—Thursday evening, remember? And you didn't think those scones Mother baked were really for you, did you? She knew you'd give them to the wanderers."

"Tea, Cruise girl." Elsie shuffled in with a sloshing cup of chamomile tea.

Elsie Weather, who until now I'd have sworn didn't know what was happening from one moment to the next.

"Pot was already going," she said.

"Ah, wonderful." Mr. Wetheral smiled. "And right on cue. Thank you, Mother."

I held the mug round the top and Elsie unhooked her knobbly fingers from the handle. She went back out to the kitchen.

"Mother sees more than you'd think. She's another that has a good eye."

"But why didn't you say anything? Why didn't you tell the mayor? You must hate the wanderers. They killed your family."

Elsie came back in with a second cup of tea. She handed it to Mr. Wetheral, then leaned on her stick and looked at me.

"Ah. Yes." Mr. Wetheral sighed. "I ought to explain about that. It wasn't wanderers that set fire to my house, Maggie."

"It wasn't? But—"

"That was a rumor that someone started. And it suited everyone to believe it." Mr. Wetheral sipped at his tea.

I balanced my mug on the arm of the chair. "What happened?"

He gave his mother a sad smile. "It was an accident, of sorts. I'll explain. I had two daughters, you see. Bella, our eldest, she wasn't like your Jed. She wasn't like you, or Lindi Chowdhry, or Beth Goodman. She didn't get enough oxygen when she was born. She ran around; she went to school. She was a gentle, loving soul, but she didn't understand things, not like other fourteen-year-olds. She needed, um, looking after."

Elsie shifted her stick from one hand to the other.

Mr. Wetheral took another sip of tea.

"What about camp? Did she still have to go?" I said.

"Well, that's where our problems really started. I couldn't let her go. I just couldn't."

Elsie took in a shaky breath. "Got to check on something," she said, and shuffled out of the room.

Mr. Wetheral waited till she'd gone.

"Mother doesn't like to be reminded of the whole business," he said. "Hurts too much, you see."

I tried my tea. It wasn't so bad today. It was kind of her to make it.

"We were going to leave town, in secret, the four of us—and Mother too, I'd hoped." Mr. Wetheral wrapped his hands round his mug, just like Elsie had held her raspberry-ade at Jed's party.

"Leave town? Beyond the boundary?"

"We were planning to find some wanderers. See if they'd help us."

"Wanderers? But wanderers are—"

"There was talk of someone else from Fennis Wick having done it, years before. Different circumstances, of course. A couple with just one child. The child had gone to camp and they couldn't bear to stay after that. So they left to become wanderers—to join others of like mind, others who couldn't abide Andrew Solsbury's system. Made a good go of it, if the stories were true. They weren't bad people. Not dirty, or dangerous, or deceitful."

"But you didn't go. You're still here—you and Mrs. Weather."

"Yes." Mr. Wetheral put his cup down beside him. "Mother feared the unknown, you see. Feared the cold winters, and the wild people. We all did, I suppose. But she refused to leave, warned us against it so much we began to doubt ourselves and fear for the girls and, well, I lost my nerve. We didn't leave. Instead, I tried to hide the four of us away the night before Bella was due to go to camp. I locked us all indoors. Bella and her little sister, Mia, and my wife, Christie, and me—I bolted the doors, boarded up the windows. We were in a different house back then—right down on the South View boundary. Christie always liked to look out beyond the town, you see." Mr. Wetheral looked out of the window into his sprawling, spreading garden. "She was Mayor Anderson's younger sister—did you know that?"

I nodded.

"But she was nothing like her at all." He stared through the window.

I took a gulp of tea.

"Anyway," he said, "I stocked up on food and water, and told them no one was going out and no one was coming in. Ridiculous, really, to even think it would work. A whole group of townspeople gathered outside, ready to carry out the eldest edict.

"*Support those who support the edict and punish those who do not*," I said.

"Exactly."

"Were they going to punish you?"

Mr. Wetheral rubbed his forehead. "I don't think so, no. They just wanted to get hold of Bella and send her to camp. They'd sent their eldests, after all."

"So how *did* the fire start?"

"Bella found some old matches in a drawer. Simple as that. It was dark. The billy lamps had run down and we couldn't charge them up again. She was trying to help. But houses burn quick. Quicker than you'd ever think. I tried to save them, Maggie." Mr. Wetheral's voice shuddered. "I tried so hard."

His whole family. Killed in the fire.

"There weren't any wanderers?"

He shook his head.

"Then why don't you tell everyone it wasn't the wanderers? It's not fair to blame them if they didn't do it."

"Oh, I did, Maggie. I said it again and again and again. It was my fault, I told them. It was all my fault. But then someone started the rumor." Mr. Wetheral pulled a handkerchief from his pocket and dabbed at his damp eyes. "I always suspected Mayor Anderson."

"Mayor Anderson?"

"She needed someone easy to blame for her sister's death, but she also needed to keep people from leaving town. Blaming the wanderers achieved both, even if it wasn't true. I don't know. Maybe I'm wrong. I'm probably wrong. But in any case, once the rumor started, no one wanted to believe anything else."

"Why not?"

"I wasn't the only one feeling guilty about the fire. All those people who were outside the house that night—they didn't help me. Not one of them. So they all preferred to believe it was wanderers to blame, rather than them letting a family burn. And if people really want to believe something, there's very little you can do to change it."

"They didn't help? They didn't try and save your family?"

I couldn't believe it. People from Fennis Wick. People I probably knew.

Mr. Wetheral rubbed his damaged hand.

"Why are you still here, Mr. Wetheral? How can you live in the same town as them?"

He picked up his tea. Sipped at it.

"It's hard to leave when you're recovering from burns on over half your body. And harder still when you have an elderly mother to care for. And then, well, there's my girls, of course. I can't leave my girls."

Those graves.

Those well-tended graves.

"But who were they, those people? You must hate them, you must—"

He shook his head again. "It doesn't matter who they were. They were scared too, just like me. Scared of the war. Scared of what they'd sent their eldests to. And there I was, refusing to send mine."

"But you couldn't have sent her, Mr. Wetheral. You couldn't have."

"I shouldn't have hidden us away either. I should have been

brave, had courage. I should have done the right thing for Bella. I should have joined the wanderers."

I pressed my fingers to my forehead. My eyes ached.

"I'm sorry, Maggie." He placed his mug back down on the table. "We have more immediate matters to deal with. Your own wanderers, beyond the hawthorn. Tell me how I can help."

~ ~ ~

I told him all about Trig's sweater. I told him how I'd met Una and how I'd helped her. I even told him about the antibiotics.

"So that's where they went to," he said.

I told him about meeting Mr. Opal and how I thought he might have been one of the wanderers who'd killed Mr. Wetheral's family but now I knew that wasn't true.

I told him about wanting to be a hero and a wanderer catcher and how I didn't even know what was right and what was wrong anymore, or who was good and who was bad.

And I told him how Mayor Anderson was taking Una to camp and how Mr. Opal said he'd already sent his eldest to camp and actually that was the main reason why I was there, because I didn't know if it was true or not.

I opened the book cover and slid out the photo and there was Felix staring up at me with his gappy grin and his yellow hair. Una's brother.

"Well, I'm glad you've stopped to take a breath, Maggie," said Mr. Wetheral. "Might I have a look?"

He turned it over. The back was blank.

"There's something written in the corner," I said. "Mr. Opal said it proved Felix had gone to camp. But it's too tiny to read."

He turned it face up again and peered into the corners. "Aha." He held up a pausing finger. He put the photo down, picked up his stick, and made his way over to the other side of the room. He rummaged through a drawer and brought something out. A something wrapped in cloth.

He sat down again, photo on his knees, and unwrapped the cloth.

It was a piece of glass, perfectly round, framed in wood. A handle stuck out from one side. He gave it a polish with its cloth, thumb on top, fingers underneath. Just like Grandad Cruise polishing his spectacles.

He held it up.

I frowned.

"It's a magnifying glass. Take a look." He hovered it over the photograph.

Felix's left eye became enormous. As the glass moved, every part of his face grew huge, then shrank again as it passed.

"Wow," I said.

"Mmm." Mr. Wetheral paused over the writing in the corner. "If you look there, you'll see that Mr. Opal was right. This is an official eldest photograph. There used to be lots of them, but it's mostly paintings now. Photography equipment's so hard to come by. But this boy definitely went to camp."

The writing was huge through the glass.

*Felix R. Opal, Eldest Bound for Glory.*

*M. M. Lombardo.*

"See? The photographer has titled and signed the image. Just like I do on my eldest portraits."

I gently moved the glass aside and tried to read it straight off the photo.

"How can the photographer have written it that small?"

"Oh, they'd have signed a much larger version. The customer must have requested a smaller copy. Easy enough to produce, if you have access to the right equipment. And a reliable power supply, of course."

"You know what this means?" My heart quivered. "It means Mr. Opal was telling the truth—Una doesn't have to go to camp."

"Indeed she doesn't."

Mr. Wetheral handed me the photo. I slid it back into *The New Poets*, tucked it safely under my arm.

I was going to get my friend back.

But.

But. But. But. If Mr. Opal had told the truth about Felix, what about the other things he'd said? Was the Quiet War really over?

"You all right, Maggie?" Mr. Wetheral wrapped the magnifying glass back up in its cloth.

"There's something else. Something Mr. Opal said."

"Mmmm? What's that?"

*No.*

*Mayor Anderson wouldn't trade our eldests, or lie to us about the war. She wouldn't.*

My rib cage hammered against *The New Poets*. Stupid Maggie-middler. Afraid again.

"Nothing," I said. "It's nothing. It's just that I have to take this photograph to the mayor now, before she takes Una to camp. And I don't want to be too late."

"Be careful what you say, Maggie." Mr. Wetheral put the glass away in the drawer. "It's best if you don't tell Mayor Anderson you went out of the boundary."

"Okay." My voice came out small.

Mr. Wetheral put his right hand on my shoulder. Ungloved. Warm.

"It's all right to feel afraid, you know." He smiled. "Being brave doesn't mean not feeling afraid. True bravery is feeling your fear, but going ahead and doing what's right anyway."

*Feeling your fear, but going ahead and doing what's right anyway.*

Like Jed and Lindi, going to camp.

# Chapter 27

Mayor Anderson opened the door, her hair loose to her shoulders.

"Maggie Cruise!" She held her arms out wide. "The hero of the hour. What can I do for you?"

*Be brave, Maggie. Feel your fear.*

"It's Una," I said, "the wanderer girl. She's not an eldest."

"S'that right, now?" She leaned on the doorframe.

"Yes. She had a brother. Much older than her. He went to camp just after she was born, so she doesn't need to go."

Mayor Anderson started tapping her fingers against her thigh. Slowly. One at a time. Littlest, ring, middle, index, thumb. *One, two, three, four, five*. Like she was learning piano.

"I've got proof," I said.

"Proof?"

*One, two, three, four, five. One, two, three, four, five.*

"Yes, look." I took out the photograph. Maybe this wouldn't be so hard after all. "This is Felix, Una's brother, see? And here, in the corner—it's the photographer's signature. It's an official eldest photograph. Mr. Wetheral checked it with his magnifying glass."

She glanced at it.

"Mr. Wetheral," said Mayor Anderson, "is the ridiculous man my sister was foolish enough to marry, and she ended up dead." She pulled a hair band off her wrist and tied her hair into a tight ponytail. "He's a coward and a dreamer. A good portrait artist, I'll grant you, but don't listen to everything he says. He's got even worse since the fire."

*Ridiculous? Mr. Wetheral?*

*A coward?*

"But, Mayor Anderson, he's—"

"But nothing, Cruise. This photograph is meaningless. And where did you get it, anyway?"

"I . . . um . . . Una gave it to me. A few days ago. It's not meaningless. It's proof. You can't take someone to—"

"Who are you to tell me what I can and can't do?" She pinched the top of the photograph and pulled it out from between my fingers. "You don't even know if this is really her brother."

"But they look exactly like each other. How could he be anyone else?"

She held it out of my reach and glared at me. "I don't see the likeness," she said.

Then she tore Felix into two pieces. Right down the middle.

"Stop!"

She put the two pieces together, one on top of the other, and tore again. "Go home, Maggie Cruise. Enjoy being the hero for a few days, get on with your schoolwork, then go and do your apprenticeship with silly old Wetheral. It's that or be out in the fields with your mother."

Again, she tore the picture. It was in eight pieces now. Mr. Opal's photograph. The one he'd kept so carefully for all those years.

She slammed the door shut, taking the torn photograph with her.

I held my hand to my mouth.

I stared at the closed front door.

She hadn't even looked at it properly.

She'd torn it up.

Why would she do that?

Why would she send someone to camp who wasn't an eldest?

I turned round.

The square didn't look square anymore. Its edges leaned toward me and the corners closed in.

And Andrew Solsbury stood in the middle and sneered.

# Chapter 28

I shook my head. Rubbed my eyes.

*Una.*

I ran out into the square and looked up at the mayor's highest window. There it was—that movement again.

*Una.*

I had to get the photograph back. Fix the bits together. If the mayor wasn't going to listen, I'd have to prove to someone else that Una wasn't an eldest.

I needed the photograph.

I scooted round the side of the mayor's house, keeping low. I crawled round the back, knelt on the damp ground, peered over a window ledge. The room was empty—just a desk and some shelves.

The window was ajar. I slid my fingers through, stretched for the inside handle. It was just out of reach. I wiggled my hand. It wouldn't go in. I shoved it harder, scraped off some skin.

My fingertips touched the handle. I pushed.

*Click.*

I checked no one was watching, then climbed inside.

~ ~ ~

The mayor's house was the exact opposite of Mr. Wetheral's. Everything was tidy, dusted, gleaming. Penny Parker, the Parker brothers' mom, went in every day, loaded up with dusting cloths and brushes. She was good at her job, for certain.

There—under the desk—a trash can. The mayor would've put the pieces of photo in a trash can, wouldn't she?

I pulled it out. Completely empty. Course it was. She wouldn't have come in here just to throw something away. It'd be in a different one most likely, somewhere else in the house.

I listened at the door. Footsteps. I flattened myself against the wall. Stupid really, I'd be squashed if anyone came in.

The footsteps went past.

I breathed out.

What were those—on that shelf? I took a step closer. Tiny golden models. Butterflies. Shiny and polished. A whole row, each one a different variety. I picked up the one on the left. It was heavier than it looked. *A peacock, I think.* Eyes on the tips of its wings. I could only identify it from the markings because there weren't any colors—every butterfly was completely gold. I looked along the row. A gatekeeper, a tortoiseshell, a brown argus, a speckled wood. And right at the end—a red admiral. Those diagonal stripes and wide pointed wings.

I put the peacock back.

My gaze wandered across the shelves. Hold on. Was that Mr. Opal's knife? On the lowest shelf? It was. I took it, untied the laces, opened the flap, ran my fingers over the carved handle.

I didn't know about the golden butterflies, but this knife wasn't the mayor's to keep. I tied it up and stuck it into the front of my pants. Pulled my shirt down over the top. I'd be returning that to Mr. Opal, same time as I returned Una.

If the knife was here, maybe the photograph was too. Maybe she hadn't thrown it away.

I opened the top drawer of the desk.

There was a stack of papers. I took them out, sat down on the chair. It was one of those ones that spin round. Lindi's dad had one just like it. I spun around a few times, then steadied myself. Picked up the first sheet of paper. Something about units and bananas. It had Saturday's date on it, September 6.

The second sheet was just loads and loads of writing. The third was the same. I flicked past. Between the third and fourth sheets was a photograph. Not Felix. It was a group of people sitting at a long table. Six of them. Celebrating. Like an eldest's birthday party, only better. There was tons of food—unusual, brightly colored. Bananas, and other fruits too. And something else I'd only ever seen in a book—a pineapple. I remembered it because we had pines in Fennis Wick, and we had apples. But we didn't have anything that looked even remotely like a pineapple.

I peered at the people—their clothes sparkled, like the sequins on Lindi's summer diary.

Wait. There was Mayor Anderson. It was definitely her. She was raising a glass of something pale and yellow toward the photographer. *Cheers!*

Is this what Mayor Anderson did when she went away—when

she took our eldests to camp, when she went on her trips to the city? Did she eat good food, drink wine, and wear sparkling clothes?

*It must be expensive—that food, those clothes. Even to have the photograph taken. Photographic equipment was hard to come by. Mr. Wetheral said so.*

So how did these people come by it?

*Corrupt officials who just can't give up on the eldest edict. They get too much from it, see?*

Mr. Opal's words echoed in my head.

*Goods she'd never be able to lay her hands on otherwise.*

I took the photograph, slid it into my back pocket. Then I read the next page.

On the left-hand side of the sheet it read:

*Thursday, August 28.*

*1 unit.*

One unit. *Could that be a person? An eldest?* Deb Merino had gone to camp on August 28—it was Mom's birthday. We had the hedgehog cake when we got home.

And on the right-hand side it read:

*200 x gas (42 lbs).*

The gas canisters.

My stomach writhed. *Did Mayor Anderson trade Deb Merino in for those blue gas canisters?*

I flipped back to the first page.

*Saturday, September 6.*

*2 units.*

Jed and Lindi.

*8 crates bananas.*

*1 figurine, red admiral, 18-ct gold.*

*Misc. textiles.*

The tiny gold butterflies. *Figurines.* The red admiral—the latest addition to Mayor Anderson's collection.

She'd traded Lindi and my brother for eight crates of bananas, a lifeless gold butterfly, and a bunch of new clothes.

Mr. Opal hadn't lied about anything. The war was over. Our eldests were being traded. For a load of stuff we didn't even need.

I leaned back. My head was heavy with the whole truth of it. The chair spun round slowly.

"Oh, Cruise." Mayor Anderson stood cross-armed in the doorway. "What did you go and do this for?"

# Chapter 29

I leaped up and headed for the window.

Lyle Parker. Looking in. His face squashed up against the glass.

The Mayor shook her head. "Things have been looking so good for you, Maggie."

I glanced at the papers. Maybe she hadn't seen what I'd been reading.

"I . . . I was just . . . I wanted to find the photo you tore up—the one of Una's brother. That's all. It doesn't belong to you, Mayor Anderson. It belongs to Una and her dad."

"Photograph? I have no idea what you're talking about."

Dirty.

Dangerous.

Deceitful.

She picked up the pile of papers from the desk. Looked over the first few sheets.

"Think you're smart, don't you, Cruise? Think you can judge me."

"It's not right." My voice came out tiny.

"What's that? Speak up, girl."

"It's not right, what you're doing, trading eldests." I was louder this time. "The war's over, isn't it? You've been lying to us."

She opened the desk drawer and dropped the papers back inside.

"You have no idea what you're talking about. The only reason half the people in this town are alive is because of me. I have a system in place that means we continue to receive essential supplies, through good times or bad."

"Essential supplies? Bananas and figurines?"

"I keep you safe, Cruise. You've got fuel for when your generators break down, and clothes to keep you warm."

"I'd rather risk dying of cold than sell my brother."

"You've lost one person, Cruise. Just one. D'you know how many I've lost? Both my sisters, my beautiful daughter—and then my mother. Do you know what she died of? *The cold*. No one should die of the cold, not in the twenty-first century. And I swore that no one else would. Not in our town. Not on my watch."

"Your daughter went years ago, when there really was a war. You sent my brother away for *bananas*. Bananas and figurines. They aren't going to keep us alive all winter."

"And clothes. Warm clothes that I'll be handing out to those who need them. I've kept my promise. I've kept everyone warm, every single winter." Mayor Anderson pressed her hands to the sides of her head. "Every single winter," she repeated.

*Warm clothes?* My fists hardened. "You think anyone's going to want to wear any of those clothes or burn any of your gas when they find out how you got them?"

Mayor Anderson sighed. "No one's going to find out, Cruise. Breaking and entering is a serious offense. Grif?" She called out to the hallway.

Grif Parker stepped in.

"Take the Cruise girl upstairs and lock her in with the other one."

Grif put a tight hand on my shoulder. "C'mon," he said. He stank of home brew.

He pushed me up a full four staircases. At the top there was a narrow landing. Neel sat on the floor in front of a closed door, picking bits out of his teeth.

"Extra one for you to guard," said Grif.

Neel opened the door and bundled me in.

~ ~ ~

It was a long loft room, with short walls and sloped ceilings. A tatty old sofa and a thin rug on the floor. Light spilled in through a skylight. The only other window was the tiny one at the end—the one that overlooked the square—the highest window in town. The one I'd seen movement in.

Una.

Where was she?

I looked through the window. The whole south of the town was spread out before me. The caravans, the vegetable plots, Frog Alley, the tops of our houses. My head swirled and my fingers gripped the window frame. I never was good at being up high.

Mrs. Gebby, outside the laundry.

"Mrs. Gebby! Mrs. Gebby!" I banged on the glass.

She couldn't hear. But maybe if I opened the window?

Even the thought made my stomach roll.

*Feel your fear, Maggie. Feel your fear.*

I got hold of the window, yanked it upward.

It wouldn't shift.

I changed position, got a better angle, yanked again.

It was jammed shut.

I banged again.

"Mrs. Gebby! Mrs. Gebby!"

What was that? A sound, from behind the sofa.

"Una? Una? Are you here?"

I ducked behind the sofa and there she was. Curled up, on her side. Just like her dad in the forest. Her hair fallen over her face.

"Una!" I knelt down beside her. "Are you okay?"

She turned her head. Her eyes were swollen with tears. "Go away," she said.

"What? No—I can help you—I can—"

"I don't want your help. I hate you, Maggie. I hate you."

"But, Una—"

"Can't you hear me? I hate you. You're the worst person I've ever met in my whole life. I didn't always believe my dad when he told me there were wicked people around, but I do now. Go away. Leave me alone."

"I didn't mean for—"

"Go away!"

I got up. Stepped back.

I looked at my hands, still stained with her dad's blood.

She was right. I was dirty, dangerous, deceitful.

Just like Mayor Anderson.

I sat down. Una was there, right behind me. Only the back of the sofa divided us.

I curled up, just like her. Knees to my chest.

A sob boiled up inside me and erupted out. And another. And another. And another.

I clutched my hands to my eyes and soaked them with tears.

# Chapter 30

*Clunk.*

The door unbolted.

I opened my eyes. Darkness. Nighttime already.

The dim light of a just-lit billy lamp swept across the sloping ceiling.

"Wanderer? Get up. Time to go."

Mayor Anderson.

Robbie stood behind her in the doorway, his own lamp throwing light onto his face.

"Time to go where?" I said.

The mayor held her lamp out at arm's length.

"Where d'you think, Cruise?"

"You're taking Una now? In the middle of the night?"

"Good a time as any. She's a wanderer. She doesn't get a send-off."

"You can't take her." I leaped up. "I won't let you."

"Where is she? What've you done with her?" Mayor Anderson looked into the corners of the room. "Wanderer? Where are you?"

"She's got a name," I said. My mouth went dry. "She's called Una."

"Here she is." Mayor Anderson held her lamp over the back of the sofa.

"Leave her alone," I said.

"What was that? How many times do I have to tell you, middler? Speak up."

"Leave her alone!" I threw myself forward and rammed her with my shoulder.

She hardly budged.

I charged again, got my elbow into her ribs.

"Ow, you little—"

Someone grabbed me from behind. Pinned my arms to my sides. Robbie.

"Shame on you for holding back an eldest, Maggie Cruise." Mayor Anderson shook her head.

I struggled against Robbie.

"What are you doing, Maggie?" he said. "She's just a wanderer. Let the mayor take her to camp. Stop making life difficult for yourself."

If I could just reach under my shirt I could grab the knife. It was still there, tucked into my pants, digging into my stomach.

I twisted and turned, but he held me solid.

"Neel? Grif?" Mayor Anderson called toward the doorway. "Come and help me get the wanderer out."

Neel and Grif loped in and pulled Una up. She was limp.

*Fight, Una, fight!*

She didn't, though. They dragged her by her elbows.

"Leave her alone!" I pulled my arms but Robbie held tight.

"Stop it, Maggie. Just stop." It was Una, eyes on the floor. "I don't want your help. I don't even want it."

"See?" said Mayor Anderson. "She doesn't appreciate your efforts. That's wanderers for you. I did try to warn you. Shame on you, Maggie Cruise, for keeping their company."

She left the room. Neel and Grif followed, pulling Una between them.

"Do yourself a favor and let it go, Maggie." Robbie loosened his grip. "Sit there and calm down." He pushed me toward the sofa.

I fell onto the seat.

"That's better," he said. "Now, don't try anything stupid. I'll be right outside on the landing." He went to the doorway, picked up his billy lamp. "Look, Maggie, Jed's only just gone to camp and, well, no one wants anything to happen to you. So keep your head low, all right? I'm sure the mayor'll let you out before long."

He closed the door quietly behind him and the room sank back into darkness.

He pulled the bolt across.

*Clunk.*

~ ~ ~

I felt for the doorknob in the blackness. I rattled it hard.

"Robbie! Robbie! You've got to let me out! They can't take

her to camp. Camp's not what you think it is. Did you know? Let me out. Please—let me out. I've got to help her."

*Bang-bang-bang.*

I thumped the door.

*Bang-bang-bang.*

"Shut up, Maggie. You're not getting out so you might as well save your energy."

I leaned my head on the wall.

I blinked. I breathed.

I could see fuzzy outlines. The doorframe, the sofa.

The sofa. It was the only thing in the room, apart from me and the rug. Could I use it to break down the door? If I lifted it up on one end? Pushed it over?

*Don't be stupid, Maggie.* It'd never work. And I'd still have Robbie to deal with.

I collapsed onto the sofa, hit my forehead with the heels of my hands.

*Think, Maggie.*

*Think.*

*Think.*

*Think.*

*Tick, tick.*

*Tick, tick.*

Grandad Cruise's watch ticked away the precious, precious minutes.

Five.

Ten.

Twenty.

Twenty-five.

Robbie coughed, still there behind the door.

It was no good. I couldn't wait any longer.

There was only one way out.

# Chapter 31

There was a wide moon and a starry sky. Peering through the tiny window, I could make out the square below me. Andrew Solsbury in the middle. The laundry on the far side.

I pressed my dry tongue to the roof of my mouth.

I had to do it.

I had to climb down.

I pulled the knife out from its sheath. Maybe I could break the glass with the handle. But Robbie would hear for sure.

I felt round the edges of the window, pushing it as I went. Which bit was sticking? The side? The bottom?

*Here*. I slid the blade in between the window and the frame. Eased it round, levered it loose. Tried lifting the window again. It creaked and groaned and—there—it opened, just a little. I tucked the knife away, shifted position, and heaved at the window one more time.

It came free. Raised right up. Cool, fresh air rushed into the room. The smell of back-garden digesters and dairy cows. The smell of Fennis Wick. I breathed it in.

Voices, down on the ground outside. Too far away for me to

hear what they were saying, but I could tell who it was. Mayor Anderson and Neel. They were round the side of the house, where the jeep was.

I didn't have much time.

~ ~ ~

I put one leg over the edge of the window. Got a foothold on the ledge below. Gripped the frame with shaky hands.

Dark ground swirled underneath me.

*Don't look down, Maggie. Never look down.*

I twisted round to face the room.

I had to get the other leg out.

Dry mouth. Pumping heart. Slipping hands.

I gripped harder.

*Don't look down.*

I leaned into the room, lifted my other leg and hooked it out of the window. Both feet on the ledge.

*Doing okay. Doing okay.*

I clung to the window frame. Hugged it with my whole body.

A cool night breeze blew up from the cemetery. It swept around my face. Brought whispers from the old, dead relatives.

*Breathe, Maggie. Breathe.*

*Climb down, Maggie, climb down.*

But my fingers were set hard. They'd never let go. Never.

*Ker-lunk. Ker-lunk.*

The jeep doors.

*Climb down, Maggie, climb down.*

I eased myself away from the window.

My stomach rolled.

*You're just a middler. Always too scared of everything.*

*Always too scared.*

I pressed myself back in.

*Stupid Maggie.*

*Always too scared.*

I couldn't do it.

There were only a few minutes now. Only a few minutes and Una would be gone. On her way to camp. And I'd be left here, a middler-shaped bundle of fear, clinging to a window frame.

Letting her down.

Letting everyone down.

My fingers ached with the gripping.

*Maybe I should just let go.*

"Get her in the jeep, Neel."

Una.

If I didn't move now, it would be too late.

*Move, Maggie, move.*

*Feel your fear.*

*Do the right thing.*

I eased myself away from the window again.

Released a foot from the ledge.

The ground spun round.

*Feel your fear.*

I placed my foot down, set it on the top of the window below.

*Do the right thing.*

I let go with my right hand, got a hold on the ledge.

Second leg down, second hand down.

Two feet firm. Two hands firm.

I stopped.

I breathed.

*Don't look down.*

*Climb, Maggie, climb.*

Foot—hand—foot—hand.

Down to the next window.

To the next ledge.

I was doing it. I was doing it.

The next window.

The next led—

My foot slipped.

I gripped harder. Caught myself.

*Feel your fear.*

The next ledge. I was there.

The next window.

The next—

My foot felt around in the inky air.

No ledge.

No window.

No nothing.

I hooked my leg back up.

There were no more footholds.

*Ter-rutt-terutt-trutt.*

The jeep.

I was going to be too late.

I was going to be too late, if I didn't do something absolutely right now.

I looked down.

The ground lurched.

I squeezed my eyes shut and squashed myself flat against the wall again.

*Ter-rutt-terutt-trutt.*

*Look down, Maggie, look down.*

I forced my eyes open and peered at the shadows underneath me.

I was above the front door with its triangular gable.

I just needed to get my foot to the middle. Then I could balance on top of the triangle and climb down from there.

*Terutt-terutt.*

*Hurry up, Maggie. Hurry up.*

I stretched my leg out.

It wouldn't reach.

I pointed my toes. Just another few centimeters. That's all it needed. Three or four centimeters.

*Churrrrrrr-utt.*

"Have a good trip." *Thwack, thwack.* Neel, giving the jeep its goodbye smacks.

I had to do it.

*Feel your fear.*

I jumped.

# Chapter 32

I hit the gable and fell forward, right off the front. A rolling, gashing crash of knees and arms and roof slates. Landed hard on the cobblestones near Mayor Anderson's front door.

Legs. Hands. Brain.

Nothing worked.

What was I doing?

*Una.*

*Una.*

*Una.*

*Got to stop the jeep.*

It turned the corner and puttered straight past me, front lights glaring on the ground ahead of it, black smoke chugging out behind.

I scrambled up and hurtled forward. I leaped for the back, got a foot onto the bumper and a hand on the roof rack. I pulled myself in close, gripped on tight, and gulped down a throatful of smoke.

*Don't choke, Maggie. Don't cough.*

A shadowed face on the inside of the window.

Una.

The jeep juddered my bones.

It carried us out of the square, northeast, toward the dairy.

The bumper was narrow, and my hands screamed from gripping.

One backward glance from the mayor and I'd be spotted.

*The roof, Maggie.*

*Got to get onto the roof.*

I bent a knee in, wedged my foot onto the door handle, and— *one, two, three*—I pushed myself up.

I squeezed in between the bars of the roof rack.

I lay on my side.

Nighttime air swooped around me.

We rattled past the dairy, along the edge of the northside fields and over the bent bridge. Then we crossed in front of the mill and drove straight through the wheat-field boundary without even a moment's wavering.

I closed my eyes and held on tight.

~ ~ ~

Mayor Anderson wound the jeep across wide roads, winding left, then right; left, then right; left, then right. Trying to dodge the bushes and roots, I s'posed, but she didn't miss them all. I got flung backward and forward, side to side, up and down. It was rockier than a ride in Mr. Chowdhry's tractor.

Trees swiped at me from both sides and blocked out the moon. I turned onto my front and made myself as flat as I could, lower than the roof rack. The branches beat on the bars, right next to my ears. The cold jeep roof vibrated underneath me.

*Breathe, Maggie. Breathe.*

Fennis Wick was behind us, getting further and further away.

Mom, Dad, and Trig, getting further and further away.

The old, dead relatives fading.

The engine chugged and spluttered.

The branches grabbed and scratched.

I swallowed, but my mouth didn't work properly. A big lump of nothing sat at the back of my tongue.

I shivered. Shoulders shaking, knees shaking, heart shaking.

~ ~ ~

The jeep slowed down, swung to the left, and stopped.

I opened my eyes, the side of my face still pressed to the roof.

Mayor Anderson got out of the jeep, holding her lamp. It glowed dull in the blackness.

I stayed still.

Cold.

Stone.

Quiet.

*Ker-lunk.* She locked the jeep door and walked away.

I blinked. The moon's glow drew dark outlines. A building. Tall windows. A van, bigger than the jeep, parked right next to us.

The smell of lavender, strong as you like.

I lifted my head.

Mayor Anderson reached the front of the building. She knocked on the door. *Clud-clud-clud.*

I stayed.

Stone.

Still.

*Clud-clud-clud.* Not a wooden door. Glass?

She cupped her hand against it and peered through.

Glass.

"Cal?" she called.

*Clud-clud-clud.*

*Clud-clud-clud.*

*Clud-clud-clud.*

A warm billy-lamp fuzz lit up inside. The dark outline of a person came to the door and fiddled with the lock.

Mayor Anderson stepped back.

"What's going on?" The person opened the door. He was wearing a pair of underpants and absolutely nothing else at all. "For heaven's sake, it's the middle of the—Tasher? Tasher Anderson? Is that you? You know it's the middle of the night?"

"I know, I know," said the mayor. "You going to let me in?"

He looked out across the driveway.

*Stone.*

*Still.*

*Maggie.*

*Stone.*

*Still.*

"All right, then," he said. "C'mon."

They went in, and closed the door behind them.

I breathed out.

~ ~ ~

I pulled myself up from under the roof rack and climbed down off the jeep. Tried the door handles. Locked.

I looked through the window. Darkness.

Una.

Where was she?

Was she on the floor, eyes squeezed tight like mine had been on the roof?

I tapped, ever so soft.

Nothing.

"Una," I whispered. "Una, it's Maggie."

Nothing.

I looked at the building. Not a house, really. Not a church, or a school. A town hall? No, not that either.

Keeping to the shadows, I edged round the jeep, then round the van, and crept toward the front door.

~ ~ ~

I crouched low. Mr. Opal's knife was still tucked into my pants. The handle dug into my stomach.

The billy lamp was brightening up inside.

". . . ridiculous. I'm not a twenty-four-hour service, y'know." The man slammed his keys down on a desk. His voice carried through a high open window. Tatty yellow posters curled on the wall behind him.

"She's a wanderer, Cal!" said Mayor Anderson. "I can't keep

her in town—she's caused enough trouble already. Anyway, I don't know what you're complaining about, she'll fetch you plenty up at the city."

*Fetch him plenty?*

The lump came back to my throat.

Cal pulled a bottle out from behind the desk, unscrewed the top, and glugged.

Mayor Anderson snatched up the keys. "I'll lock her up myself then—I don't need any help."

She took a few quick strides to the front door and opened it wide. I scooted sideways.

"Where d'you want her?" she called back.

Cal sighed good and loud. "All right. Number nine's free. S'pose I'd better go up and get some clothes on. Then we can talk trade. No new stock since the weekend, though, so don't get your hopes up. You won't be getting any more bananas."

Mayor Anderson trudged out to the jeep, billy lamp swinging at her side.

*Hold on.*

*She'll see me when she comes back.*

*She'll see me for absolutely certain.*

*Breathe, Maggie.*

*Breathe.*

I looked back through the glass front door. Cal was gone. The room was dark. Just the dim outline of the desk hunched on the floor.

The desk that was big enough to hide behind.

Mayor Anderson opened the back of the jeep. "C'mon then, wanderer. We're here. Time to get out."

*Feel your fear, Maggie.*

I breathed in the lavender. It smelled just like walking into our larder back home.

I stood up, stepped inside the door, and ducked under the desk.

# Chapter 33

*Clank-clink-clattle!* I crashed into a whole pile of billy lamps stacked up on the floor.

*Shush, lamps! Shhhh! Please, shhhh!*

I steadied them till they fell silent.

*Breathe.*

*Breathe.*

*A whole pile of billy lamps? Who has a whole pile of billy lamps behind their desk?*

You only get one when you're born, and you'd better look after it because there isn't another one coming your way anytime soon.

Who would've left their lamps here?

"Inside, girl." Mayor Anderson pushed someone in through the door. I peered round the side of the desk.

Una.

Head hanging, shoulders drooped.

She looked up, ever so slightly.

She caught my eye.

She didn't jump.

She didn't smile.

She didn't do anything at all.

There were two doors, one either side of the desk. They both had tiny oblong windows halfway up. Mayor Anderson had a good grip on Una's arm with one hand, her lamp and the keys in the other. She kicked one of the doors open and shoved Una through.

The door swung shut behind her and sank me into darkness again, except for a little chunk of billy-lamp light coming back through the window.

I crawled out from under the desk. Peered through to where Mayor Anderson was. It was a corridor with a whole load more doors. Mayor Anderson picked out a key from the bunch and opened a door on the left. She pushed Una inside.

I dodged down next to the lamps.

Mayor Anderson came back in. She dropped the keys on top of the desk and sat on it. It creaked. I held my breath.

She huffed.

She tapped her fingers on the desk.

*One, two, three, four, five.*

*One, two, three, four, five.*

Her billy lamp lit up the wall behind. CHIFFERTON CONSTAB-ULARY, said the words across the top. *Constabulary?* Was this an old police station?

The lamplight shone on the curling ancient posters underneath.

ELDESTS! blared one of them. YOUR COUNTRY NEEDS YOU.

ARE YOUR NEIGHBORS FOLLOWING THE EDICT? BETTER TO SPY THAN TO DIE!

BRING YOUR LAMP AND COME TO CAMP. THE BEST TIME YOU'LL EVER HAVE!

ELDESTS——KEEP THE WAR QUIET AND THE FAMILY SAFE!

WORK THE LAND——LEND A HAND

And, tucked down at the bottom: WANDERERS ARE SQUANDERERS.

Mayor Anderson huffed some more.

*One, two, three, four, five.*

*One, two, three, four, five.*

She got up, took her lamp, and went through the second door, on the other side of the desk.

Darkness.

Alone.

*Did she take the keys?*

I reached up.

I patted the desktop.

I felt around.

Nothing . . .

Nothing . . .

*There!*

Something lumpy. Metally. Spiky.

I pulled the keys down and grabbed a billy lamp off the pile.

~ ~ ~

My lamp glowed in the corridor.

I walked past the doors, quiet and soft.

There were sounds.

Murmuring.

Praying?

Crying.

And something else. Humming? No—singing, soft as you like.

I carried on past.

There. A small brassy nine on a door to the left. I knelt down, held the keys up to the lamp and searched through them. They had numbers etched into them.

Here, number nine.

I opened the door.

"Una! It's me—it's Maggie!"

She didn't leap up.

She didn't smile.

She didn't do anything at all.

"Come on." I got hold of her arm, good and tight.

Just like Mayor Anderson.

"We've got to get out." I pulled her up.

The window at the end of the corridor was still dark. We tip-toed toward it. Soft, soft, soft.

But listen.

That singing again.

Ever so quiet.

Ever so soft.

> *"In the southside fields where the clover grows*
> *I'm calling out for my Evie-oh."*

"Gray Willow." It was coming from door number two.

*"Can she hear me now? Can she see the fields?*
*Under the shadow of the gray willow."*

I knew that voice.

Been hearing that voice since I was knee-high.

Lindi.

I scrabbled with the keys.

Number eight, number ten, number three—where was two? Where was it? I dropped them onto the stone floor—*cher-clink!*

I scooped them back up again.

Number four, number one—here—number two.

I pushed it into the keyhole.

~ ~ ~

Lindi blinked in the sudden light.

There was someone else there—lying on the floor, head in her lap. She was stroking his hair.

"Jed!" I dropped onto my knees. "Is he okay?" I grabbed his hand. "Are you all right, Jed? Lindi? Is he okay?"

Lindi stared at me. "What . . . How are you here, Maggie? How did you find us?"

"Is Jed okay? What's wrong with him?"

Lindi looked down to her lap. "He tried to stop them pushing me around. They hit him. Here, right across his eye." She smoothed her hand over his forehead.

I held up the lamp and peered at Jed. He scrunched up his face and turned away.

"And we haven't had anything to eat in ages," she said. "I don't think this is camp, Maggie. I think Mayor Anderson's been lying to us."

"She's been lying for years." I glanced into the corridor. "There isn't any camp. She's just brought you here to sell you. Look, we have to be quick. Can we get Jed up? Jed? Jed? Can you hear me? It's Maggie. We've got to go."

"Mmmm?" Jed peeped through hardly open eyelids. "Magsie? That you? What's going on, Magsie?"

"Come on, Lindi. Let's get him up." I shoved the keys and the lamp into one hand and pulled Jed's arm round my shoulder. Lindi wobbled to a stand. Her hair hung limp. She got hold of Jed's other arm.

Una stepped in from the doorway.

"Who's that?" Lindi stumbled back. "Who are you? Get away—leave us alone."

"It's all right, Lindi," I said. "This is Una—she's my friend."

Una looked at me.

She didn't smile.

She took Jed's arm from Lindi and the four of us hobbled out of the room. We went through the door at the end of the corridor and rested at the desk.

"The mayor'll be back any moment," I whispered. "We have to find somewhere to hide."

"But where, Maggie?" said Lindi. "I don't even know where we are."

*Where?*

*Where can we hide?*

*Think, Maggie, think.*

*The jeep? We could get down on the floor inside, or climb on top, and get driven all the way home. But the inside would be all locked up, and we'd never be able to hide four of us on the roof.*

*Think, Maggie.*

*Think.*

*The van.*

It was bigger than the jeep, and I had Cal's keys.

*The van key must be on there somewhere.*

"There's a van outside," I said. "We'll hide in the back. Quick!"

"Magsie? Magsie?" Jed slurred my name.

"Shush, Jed." I spoke close to his ear. "Keep quiet. We're hiding."

We helped him outside.

Moonlight pooled on the jeep and the van. We made our way over.

"Oh! Fresh air!" Lindi breathed in big deep breaths. "Fresh air and lavender!" She stood a bit more upright, a bit more strong.

"Lindi," I said, "d'you think you can take Jed for a moment?"

Lindi and Una steadied Jed while I searched through the keys.

*There must be one for the van here somewhere.*

"What the . . . Cruise? *Maggie Cruise?*"

I froze. Solid. Still.

Mayor Anderson stood in the front door, her mouth wide open just like Trig. Billy lamp swinging by her side.

"How on earth . . ." She looked around. "Hang on, how did you get here? But how did you get out of the—"

"Maggie!" said Lindi. "Find the key!"

The key. The key. The key. Where was it?

*What does a van key even look like?*

"Doesn't matter." Mayor Anderson walked toward us. "I don't need the details right now. I'm impressed, though, if I'm honest. Didn't know you had it in you. Shame on me, eh? Underestimating a middler."

"Maggie!" Lindi again.

I fumbled with the keys.

Mayor Anderson looked over my shoulder at the others. "Me and you, Maggie Cruise, we've got a lot in common, you know."

Dirty.

Dangerous.

Deceitful.

"We don't have anything in common," I said.

"Oh, come on. We're both middlers. We've both got a heroic older sibling—most of the time, anyway," she glanced at Jed, "and a useless younger one."

"Trig's not useless." I spat the words.

"We're both prepared to sacrifice others in our efforts to get noticed."

"That's not true," I said. "That's not me. Not anymore."

Mayor Anderson smiled. Her billy lamp lit up her chin and the underside of her nose. "Give me the keys." She held out her hand. "Give me the keys and we'll lock these three up again. Me and you together. Then I'll drive you back home in the jeep, and you know what? Forget being Mr. Wetheral's apprentice—you can be my apprentice. You can help me keep everyone safe and warm and fed. I've been doing it for years but I can't keep going forever. The town needs someone with guts, Cruise. The town needs you."

She stepped closer, nodded at the keys. "Give them to me."

"Don't, Maggie." Lindi was right at my shoulder. "Pass them back here."

"Cal'll be down soon," said Mayor Anderson. "If he catches you like this, he won't only lock those three up—he'll lock you up too. You're not going to get anywhere by hiding in his van. You can't even drive. Come on. Just give me the keys."

I hooked my lamp over my wrist and looked down at the bunch of keys. The one nearest to me was different from all the others. Flatter than a normal key. Smaller. *That must be it. Can't believe I didn't see it before.* I picked it out.

Mayor Anderson was right, though. I couldn't drive us home. We weren't going to get anywhere. Cal'd get us out, one way or another.

Mayor Anderson nodded at her open hand.

*Feel your fear, Maggie.*

*Feel your fear, and do the right thing.*

I passed the keys back to Lindi—the small flat one separated from the rest. She whipped them away.

Mayor Anderson closed her fingers on her empty palm.

The keys jangled.

*Ker-lunk.* The van was open.

"What's going on?" Jed groaned.

"We're getting into this van," said Lindi. "C'mon."

Mayor Anderson drew herself up. She was a full head and shoulders taller than me.

The knife.

Mr. Opal's knife.

I pulled it from the front of my pants, slipped it out of the sheath and held it forward with two shaky hands. I pointed it right at the mayor. The light from our billy lamps glimmered on the blade.

"You're not locking any of them up, not ever again." I stepped back toward the van.

"*Shame upon any who refuse to send their eldests to camp,*" said the mayor. "*Shame upon them and their kin.* Remember that, Cruise?"

"Camp doesn't even exist anymore." The knife shook in my trembly fists.

Mayor Anderson stuck out her jaw. "Even so, I'd be pretty worried about my kin right now, if I were you. After all, there are wanderers near Fennis Wick, and they've a reputation for setting family homes on fire. We wouldn't want the Cruise house to be next on their list, would we?"

"Tash? Tasher?" It was Cal in the doorway, all properly dressed now.

"Cal," said the mayor. "Some kids out here got ahold of your keys. I'm going to have to leave you to it, I'm afraid—got an urgent job needs doing back home." She looked me right in the eye. "Don't worry, though, Cal—they won't get far. Lock them all up when you've caught them. You can have the fourth one for free." Mayor Anderson hurried over to the jeep, jumped inside, and turned on the engine.

*I'd be pretty worried about my kin right now, if I were you.*

"What the—Tasher? Tasher!" Cal ran out. "Where are you going? Who's got my keys?"

Mom, Dad, Trig. Back home in Fennis Wick.

I had to get to them.

I had to get home.

"Quick, Maggie—get inside!" Lindi yanked me into the van by my sweater and slammed the door shut behind me.

# Chapter 34

Cal rattled the handle.

*Thud! Thud! Thud!* He banged on the side. "Get out of my van. Get out! And hand over those keys." *Thud! Thud! Thud!*

The tinny walls shook.

"What are these?" Shadowy crates were piled up on both sides. Lindi stuck her hand inside one and pulled out a bunch of bananas.

It wasn't only Mayor Anderson who'd been lying then. Cal hadn't run out of bananas at all. I held up the lamp. *Must be nearly twenty crates' full.*

*Thud! Thud! Thud!*

The banging beat into my head.

"Is it some kind of plant?" Lindi turned the bananas upside down.

"They're bananas," I said. "Fruit. Eat one—you'll feel better. Look." I put the billy lamp down in the middle of the floor, tucked Mr. Opal's knife away, then tore a banana from Lindi's bunch. I peeled it open, just like Mom had shown me.

*Thud! Thud! Thud!*

I offered the banana to Jed. He could barely lift his arm.

"Take it," I said. "It'll make you feel better."

*Thud! Thud! Thud!*

"Get out of my van!"

Lindi peeled a banana too.

Una watched.

*Thud! Thud! Thud!*

The banging echoed round my ribs.

"We've got to get back to Fennis Wick," I said. "Mom and Dad and Trig—I've put them all in terrible danger.

*Thud! Thud! Thud!*

"I don't know what to do." I picked at my thumbnail. "We've got a van but we can't drive and if we don't get back to—"

"Hold on." Lindi spoke through a mouthful of banana. "Who says we can't drive? Pass me that lamp." She took the keys and the billy lamp and crawled over the crates to the front of the van.

"Get out!" Cal snarled through the dark window. "You think I haven't got spare keys?" *Thud! Thud! Thud!*

Lindi climbed over the back of the driver's seat and sat down. "I used to sit in Dad's tractor all the time," she called back. "He let me do the controls. Can't be that much different, can it? Look, this is where the key goes. Just got to turn it—"

*Trrrrrrrrrrut.* The engine stuttered.

She tried again.

*Trrrrrrrrrrrut.*

*Thud! Thud! Thud!*

I crawled forward, leaned over the seat, looked out of the window. The trees were outlined against the sky, but the road was a blur of darkness.

*Trrrrrrrrrrut.*

A whole panel of buttons and dials spread out behind the steering wheel. *One of them must turn the lights on.* I scanned across them. *That one, there, with the picture of a beam.* I leaned over Lindi and pressed it. The driveway lit up. Cal twisted his head away from the glare.

"Brilliant—thanks, Maggie," said Lindi.

"Right—that's it," Cal shouted through the window. "I'm going to get the spare keys. Stupid kids."

The van had mirrors on each side. I could see him and his lamp disappearing back into the police station.

Lindi turned the key again.

*Trrrrrrrrrrut.*

The engine stuttered.

"Hurry up, Lindi. Please hurry up." I squeezed the back of the seat. Cal was going to get us. He was going to get us for sure.

"Hang on," said Lindi. "Maybe if I . . ."

*Grrrrrrowl.* The engine caught.

"There!" she said. "Now, pedal down and here we go!"

The van jerked forward. A crate of bananas slid into me. Jed moaned.

The engine stopped.

"Heck." Lindi turned the key again.

*Grrrrrrowl.*

"But . . ." Lindi's hands slid to the bottom of the wheel. "We can't just leave."

The engine hummed and spluttered.

"What d'you mean, we can't leave? Lindi, we have to!" I looked in the side mirror. Cal—coming out of the front door. "He's coming back! We have to go *now*! Hurry up, Lindi! Hurry up!"

"But what about the others?" she said.

"What others?"

Cal loped toward us.

"The other eldests, in the other cells."

The murmuring, the crying. All those rooms down the corridor.

Eldests.

The whole place was full of locked-up eldests.

"I can't leave them, Maggie."

"We'll come back for them," I said. "After we've made sure everything's all right back home."

"But—"

"We'll come back, I promise we will—but we've got to go now. Go!"

Cal was huge in the mirror. He grabbed the door handle, right next to Lindi.

*Ker-lunk.* He unlocked the door.

"Go!"

Lindi put two hands on the wheel. The van lurched forward— and kept going.

Cal opened the door, ran alongside us.

"Faster!" I gripped the back of the seat.

The van jolted.

Cal got thrown off.

*Perdunk.*

The van bumped.

"AHHHHH!" Cal's voice, from outside.

Lindi leaned out, grabbed the door, and slammed it shut.

I looked in the mirror. Cal was on the ground, holding his foot, his billy lamp rolling by his side.

Faster.

Faster.

Cal stood up. He hopped after us, still clutching his foot. Getting further and further away.

Smaller.

And smaller.

And smaller.

"You did it, Lindi," I whispered. "You did it."

Cal was too small to see anymore.

"Do you think he'll be okay?" I said.

"He'll live."

*He'll live.*

*She's right.*

"We have to get back to Fennis Wick now," I said. "Fast as you can."

Lindi gripped the steering wheel, eyes on the road. "Yeah, I know, but there's a problem, Maggie."

"A problem?"

"Uh-huh. I have absolutely no idea how to get there."

*No idea how to get there.*

*Neither have I.*

*We're lost.*

*Completely lost.*

*We won't get back in time.*

*We'll be too late.*

"I can get you home." Una. It was the first thing she'd said to me since we'd been shut in Mayor Anderson's loft room.

She was standing in the back of the van, steadying herself on a banana crate.

"You can?" I said.

She scrambled forward. "Yeah. We came up an old highway. There's quite a few of them around. Number Three, my grandad called this one. We've traveled on it loads of times." She didn't smile.

"You've traveled on it?" Lindi swerved the van. Crates slipped sideways. "What does she mean, she's traveled on it?"

I looked at Una. "Can you really get us back to Fennis Wick?"

"Course. A wanderer never goes anywhere without memorizing the route they took. You never know when you might need to get out again in a hurry."

"Hold on—she's a wanderer?" Lindi twisted round. The van swerved again.

"Yes. And she's my friend," I said.

"I'm not your friend," said Una. "Not anymore." She climbed

over the front seat and sat down next to Lindi. "There's going to be a turn soon, on the right. You need to take it."

I slid down onto the van floor between the crates.

*Of course she doesn't want to be my friend. I handed her over to the mayor. Got her home destroyed and her dad beaten up.*

Mr. Opal. I still had his knife.

I pulled it out from the front of my pants.

"Here." I knelt up and passed it to Una. "Your dad's knife. It doesn't belong to me. You should have it."

"Is that a good idea, Maggie?" Lindi kept her eyes ahead. "I mean, if she's a—"

"She's a good person," I said. "The best."

Una took the knife.

"Maggie? S'that you?" Jed sat up, tried to stand. "Where's Lindi? Where is she? Where's Lindi?"

"Sit down, Jed," I called over. "Lindi's fine. She's up here, driving the van."

He collapsed back down. "Driving? Driving where? Aaaaargh." He held his head. "I've got the worst headache."

"Here." I pulled another banana from the nearest crate and crawled back to him. "I'll get you some more to eat."

"Thanks, Maggie." He rolled onto his side. "Then can you tell me what on earth is going on?"

"Yeah," I said. "Okay."

I looked out through the window at the back of the van. A pink line shimmered across the treetops in the distance. The darkness was starting to lift.

I sat down next to Jed. Una said something to Lindi, and pointed ahead. Couldn't tell what she was saying—all I could hear was engine noise—but Lindi nodded and steered the van jerkily round to the right.

I peeled the banana, broke it in two, and passed half of it to Jed.

*Drive fast, Lindi.*

*Fast as you can.*

*I need to get home.*

~ ~ ~

"Look." Lindi peered ahead. "Is that Fennis Wick?"

I scrambled forward.

Thick smoke billowed up against the pale morning sky.

Fire.

Mom. Dad. Trig.

"It's our house," I said. "Mayor Anderson's set fire to our house. Quick, Lindi. Quick!"

Lindi raced the van into town, past the mill and the fields and the dairy, into the square. She screeched past the laundry and swung to a stop round the corner.

Jed stood up in the van, all wobbly. "I'm coming. Don't worry, Maggie; I'll save them. I'll save them."

His knees buckled underneath him and he crumpled to the floor.

I flung open the back door, stepped over him, and leaped out.

# Chapter 35

Our house—groaning and roaring with flames and heat and smoke. The roof—buckled and broken. People—gathered along the road in dressing gowns and boots.

"Mom! Dad! Trig!" I screamed their names. "Let me through, let me through!"

Mom was slumped on the ground. Dr. Sunita bent over her. Dad sat next to them, coughing.

"Mom! Mom!"

"Maggie!" Dad's voice croaked. "Where have you been? Neel told us you were doing a job for the mayor but—you've been gone all night."

"Doesn't matter, Dad. I'm fine. But Mom—is she okay? And Trig?"

"They're all going to be okay, Maggie." The doctor looked up. "Mr. Wetheral saw the smoke and banged on the door. Woke them up just in time."

"Where's Trig, Dad? I can't see him." I twisted round. Where was he?

"It's okay, Maggie. Mom got him out. He's here." He cast an arm out to the side.

No Trig. I turned and craned and squinted. There were people from the school, people from the fields, people from the dairy—even Frederick was there—but no Trig.

"He's not here, Dad! Where is he? Trig! Trig!" I pushed Beth Goodman and little Devvy Chowdhry out of the way.

"Maggie!" It was Una, right behind me. "Is that him?" She pointed toward the house.

There was Trig, his sweater pulled up across his mouth, running in through the open front door.

Flames slurped and spat through the windows.

"Trig!" Dad yelled. He staggered up and stumbled over, clutching his chest, coughing. "What's he doing? Trig! Someone stop him!"

A hand grabbed mine. A warm hand. Strong. Dirty. Free.

Una.

"I have to go in," I told her.

"Course you do," she said. "What are we waiting for?"

*Feel your fear, Maggie. One more time. Feel your fear.*

We wrapped our free arms across our mouths and ran into the house together.

~ ~ ~

My eyes closed against the hot, thick blackness. The fire fizzed and crackled. I breathed in stale breath through the sleeve of my sweater. Breath that had been through my lungs once, twice, three times. Every bit of me wanted to run back outside.

*Keep calm, Maggie, keep calm. Focus on Una's hand, snug and tight.*

I squeezed. She squeezed back.

"Trig! Trig!" The air scorched at my throat. "Trig? Where are you?"

*CREAAAAAAK.*

The house let out a juddering, dying cry.

"We have to be quick!" shouted Una.

"Trig! Trig! Come out! You've got to get out!"

*CRAAAAAAAACK.*

"Jed! Jed! Jed!"

It was Trig.

Calling for *Jed?*

"C'mon, Jed, c'mon!"

He was in the sitting room. With the portrait. The Real Jed. Of course he was.

"Trig—you can leave it. Jed's home—he's home!"

I felt my way through and pulled Una with me.

Less smoke in here.

I opened my eyes a sliver.

Outlines in the dark. Trig, tugging the heavy frame. The Real Jed, half off the wall.

"Come on, Jed. *Come on.*" Trig spluttered and coughed and yanked at the picture.

The frame banged back against the wall.

"Jed! Jed!" Trig turned to face us through the smoke. "Make him come, Maggie, make him come."

I lunged forward, grabbed Trig's shoulder. "Jed's home, Trig. We don't need the portrait anymore."

He pulled away. "Don't lie, Maggie." He stopped fighting with the painting. "I'm staying with him. I won't leave him on his own."

He rested his head against the Real Jed. Pressed a palm against it.

He gasped lungfuls of smoke-filled air.

I gripped the frame. "Get the other side, Trig. We'll do it together."

*GRRRRRRAAASH.*

A groaning, leering crash from the hallway.

"Hurry up!" Una leaped across and grabbed the bottom.

Together we lifted it and slid it off the hook. Funny, but it didn't seem heavy anymore. It was light as a feather.

The smoke thickened.

"This way!" Una guided the picture toward the hallway.

The stairs had collapsed—all smashed and burning right there on the floor. The heat seared our skin.

"Close your mouths and shut your eyes," Una screamed.

All four of us—Trig and Jed and Una and me—edged through the gloom, out into the freshness.

Someone strong, someone silent, lifted Jed from us and took him to safety.

Frederick.

We fell coughing into neighbors' arms.

~ ~ ~

"Cruise girl? Cruise girl?"

Elsie. Elsie Weather.

Curled, bony fingers stroked at my cheek.

"You all right, Cruise girl?"

"She's opening her eyes, Mother, look."

Shadowed faces, old and damaged and kind, looking down on me.

"She's back with us, Mother. I told you she'd be okay."

Elsie didn't smile. She nodded. And smeared a tear away from her eye.

*Fire.*

*Trig.*

*Trig and Una.*

I sat up.

"Trig? Una? Where are they? Where are Trig and Una? Are they okay?"

"Careful, Cruise girl. Careful of your lungs."

"They're fine, Maggie. The fire's under control, and everyone's all right." Mr. Wetheral leaned out of the way. "See?"

There was Trig, just an arm's length from me, coiled up in Dad's hug.

My breathing calmed.

And Una, walking toward me.

She was all right.

She was all right.

I pushed myself up. "Thank you, Mr. Wetheral. Thank you, Mrs. Weather. I'm sorry, but I just have to—"

"Don't you worry about us." Mr. Wetheral brushed down his sleeves. "You go and see your friend. It'll take us a few minutes to get ourselves up off our knees again anyway, won't it, Mother? Go on."

I ran to Una. Threw my arms round her.

Dirt.

Sunshine.

And unwashed hair.

All still there, underneath the stink of smoke.

"I'm going to take you home," I said. "Back to your dad."

She squeezed me, hard, hard, hard. Like she was going to keep hugging forever. "I haven't got a home anymore, Maggie. I haven't got a dad. He's gone."

Gone?

I pulled away from her, found her hands and held them fast. Looked her straight in the eye.

"What d'you mean? Gone where?"

"He's dead, Maggie." A fat tear slid down her face. "Your mayor—she told those men to kill him. And then she took me back to her house."

She thought he was dead. Ever since Saturday—she'd thought her dad was dead.

"No. No! He's not dead, Una. He's alive. I've seen him."

She stared at me.

"I saw him—while you were at the mayor's house. He told me about your brother. About Felix. He told me about everything. He's alive, Una. He was mending his glasses and taking the antibiotics and fixing the Cleercan." I squeezed her hands harder. "He's alive. Really he is."

Her mouth moved, but no words came out.

"Alive, is he?" A voice behind me. "Parkers made a hash of it, I suppose."

Mayor Anderson.

~ ~ ~

"Keep away from her." I stood strong, in between Una and the mayor.

"KEEP AWAY!" I said it again, shouted it, loud as you like.

Everyone turned. Dad, Dr. Sunita, Mr. Wetheral. Teachers, dairy workers, eldests, youngests, middlers. Everyone who'd come to help or to gawp. They all turned toward us.

Mayor Anderson looked down at the ground. Shook her head. "We've seen a terrible thing happen in Fennis Wick this morning. Disaster has been avoided only by the quick actions of our very own Han Wetheral. And I have to confess"—she held up her hands—"this near disaster is partly my own fault."

Her own fault? Was she going to tell the truth?

"It's my fault because I brought a wanderer—a dirty, dangerous, deceitful wanderer—into our town." She looked at Una.

The crowd whispered. *Is she the wanderer? Is that her?*

"And Maggie Cruise—a confused middler—set the wanderer free in the early hours of this morning, and very nearly paid a terrible price for doing so. I apologize to you all, and I promise that I will remove this wanderer girl—"

"Her name's Una," I said.

"I will remove this wanderer girl *and arsonist*," continued the mayor, "from our town immediately."

The crowd bulged forward. *Arsonist. Wanderer. Murderer.*

I stepped in front of Una. "No one's taking her anywhere." I said it loud and clear. "It's not true—Una didn't set our house on fire—Mayor Anderson did. Una just helped me save Trig—you all saw it."

"That's absurd." The mayor tapped her fingers on her leg. *One, two, three, four, five. One, two, three, four, five.* "Look, it's been a long night. It's time everyone went home. I've got the jeep waiting in the square to take the wanderer to camp and I'm sure none of you want to hold me up."

"She's lying," I said. "About everything. Una's not dangerous, and camp doesn't exist anymore. The Quiet War finished years ago."

"That's ridiculous." The spidery veins on Mayor Anderson's face grew redder.

I swallowed. "Mayor Anderson's taking our eldests away and trading them in for oil and clothes and bananas and tiny little statues. I can prove it. Look." I pulled the photograph from my pocket. Mayor Anderson with her food and her sequins. *Cheers!* "This is what she does when she goes to the city." I held it up.

"Mags? Magsie?" It was Dad, calling out from the front, all soft and gentle. "It's been a long night, love. It's been a hard week. Perhaps we'd better let Mayor Anderson take the girl and—"

"No!" A voice shouted from the back of the crowd.

Lindi.

Everyone turned round.

"You should listen to Maggie," she said. "There's no such thing as camp anymore."

"Lindi! My Lindi!" Mrs. Chowdhry struggled toward her through the people.

The crowd made space for her, their mouths open and their eyes wide. Half went left and half went right, and there was Lindi standing tall, helping Jed to stay upright.

"Jed?" Dad's voice was hardly more than a whisper. "Is that Jed?"

"Una—the wanderer—she's done nothing wrong." Jed spoke in a wobbly voice. "She was with us when the fire started. Maggie rescued all three of us and brought us home. She's our hero."

"Mayor Anderson?" said Dad. "Is this true?"

"It's not how it sounds. It's not how it sounds at all." Mayor Anderson rubbed her red face even redder. "I care for you—all of you. I bring you gas, food, clothes. Do you remember how cold it was, winter before last? We wouldn't all have survived without the things I—"

"Are you trying to tell us that you've been doing us a *favor? By selling our children?*" Sally Owens's mom pushed to the front.

The whole crowd bristled and growled.

Mr. Owens shouldered past his wife. Clenched his fists into hard, trembling rocks.

It wasn't Una that needed protecting now. It was Mayor Anderson.

I stepped between her and the crowd.

Stood right in the middle.

"Don't hurt her," I said. "No one else gets hurt today. Lock her up, if you like. But no more hurting. Listen, everyone. There are better things we need to be doing."

The crowd strained to see me, peered over shoulders, squeezed between elbows. They were listening—to me, Maggie-middler. They were listening really close.

"I'm leaving town, soon as I can. I'm going back out to help all the other eldests who were locked up with Jed and Lindi, just like I promised. Then I'm going on to the city to bring back as many eldests from Fennis Wick as I can find. And anyone who wants to come along is very welcome to join me."

The crowd roared. They surged forward, got hold of me, and lifted me up. Just as if I was an eldest. Just as if I was special.

"Mag-gie! Mag-gie! Mag-gie!" they chanted. "Mag-gie! Mag-gie! Mag-gie!"

# Wednesday,
# September 10

# Chapter 36

Mom. Tucked up tight in Lindi's bed till she got better. Or till Dad found us somewhere new to live.

She'd been bathed and mended. Cleaned and kissed. Plumped and fluffed and wrapped up warm in lacy, frilly Chowdhry bedclothes. She hardly even looked like Mom anymore. I closed my eyes and buried my face into her. She still smelled of the muddy fields of Fennis Wick, though. You couldn't wash that off. It was dug into her skin.

She had one arm stuck out from under the cover and was holding onto Jed's hand, tight as you like. He was munching on his millionth piece of goldie pie. *S'all I really needed*, he'd said. *That and a glass of raspberry-ade*. He had a black eye, just as purple as Lindi's were a week ago.

"Well." Dr. Sunita put her medical bag on the end of the bed and buttoned it up. "She'll need to be well cared for over the next couple of weeks, but this is one patient I'm not worried about— she's clearly in excellent hands."

Trig pushed me out of the way. "She's got to have space to

breathe, Maggie. Dr. Sunita said so, didn't you, Dr. Sunita? S'important." He pulled Mom's covers straight. "D'you need some more water, Mom? I can hold it up for you. You're only allowed sips, though. Dr. Sunita said so. And Dad said it too. Didn't you, Dad?"

"That's right." Dad nodded. "Got to listen to Trig. He's planning on being a nurse like his old dad when he leaves school, and a great job he'll make of it too."

Mom groaned. "Maggie, Jed—you can't leave me here with these two. They'll nurse me to death." Her voice croaked and graveled. "Can't even glug down a glass of water without someone scolding me." She threw me a wink.

"Got to let your lungs recover," said Trig.

"Absolutely," said Dr. Sunita.

*Excellent hands.* The doctor was right. No need to worry about Mom. Dad and Trig'd be on her like hawks. And Mrs. Chowdhry too.

She'd get better soon as you like.

She'd have to, or they'd drive her la-la.

"We're all set." Mr. Chowdhry leaned in through the doorway. "You ready, Maggie? Jed?"

"I'm still not sure this is a good idea." Dad squeezed my shoulders. "Jed could hardly walk yesterday and—"

"We have to go, Dad," I said. "Soon as we can. All those eldests are still locked in."

"My little Maggie." He pulled me close, hugged me tight.

"Don't worry, Dad," I said. "We've got loads of help. Una's

coming, and Mr. Opal, and some others too. We're not on our own."

"Course we're not." Jed wiped the pie crumbs off his face with his sleeve. Grandad Cruise's watch glinted on his wrist. "Half the town's waiting outside—they're ready to follow Maggie anywhere. Look through the window."

There they were. A long line of ponies and carts, people from all over town. The whole Merino family. Old Doddy Stanbury. Mr. Webster. Mr. and Mrs. Owens. The Rickard sisters with their violins. Frederick, reading his book in the back of a cart. And Lindi, of course, saving a space right next to her for Jed.

All of them, waiting there in the street.

Waiting for me.

Even Mayor Anderson was there, wedged between Peg Goodman and Mr. Temple. She was going to help us track down the eldests, like it or not.

"Wow," said Trig. "There're hundreds of them. One, two, three . . ."

"And," croaked Mom, "Mr. Opal has personally promised me he'll teach Jed and Maggie everything he knows about keeping safe while you're wandering."

"Mr. Opal should be staying put." Dr. Sunita swung her bag off the bed. "That leg of his'll get better much quicker with rest and recuperation. I've told him that, but he doesn't take the slightest bit of notice."

"Can't bear to stay in one place now, that's what he told me," said Jed. "Happens to a lot of wanderers, he says."

"Eighteen!" Trig beamed. "Eighteen ponies and eighteen carts!"

Mom held out a hand to Dad. "Maggie's going to bring the eldests home. She's got plenty of help. And someone's got to stay here and make sure there are still fields and cows and crops for them to come back to."

Fields and cows and crops.

I was leaving everything. Everything I knew and loved and trusted.

My chest *gadump*ed.

Dad sighed. "Yup. Okay. C'mon, then. Finish up your good-byes. I'll come out and see you off."

I buried my head into Mom again. Smudged her bedclothes with my tears. She ran her hand through my hair.

Her heart beat under my ear. I breathed in time.

*In. Out. In. Out. In. Out.*

*Feel your fear, Maggie. Feel your fear.*

*In. Out. In. Out.*

"Oh, Maggie, get off. You're messing up the sheets again," said Trig.

~ ~ ~

We were using Mayor Anderson's cart, and Melissa, the piebald pony.

Mr. Opal sat on my left. His hair was all washed, his leg was all splinted up, and he had a brand-new bottle of trellicillin in his inside pocket.

"We'll have you digging fire holes before you know it, Maggie," he said.

Una was on my right, wearing a clean, new green gingham dress. One of Lindi's. A bit big maybe, but that was all right. Just meant it'd last her for longer. She tucked her hair behind her ears. It fell straight back out again.

Melissa snorted as she walked. We were heading through the butterfly fields—best route out for a horse and cart, according to Mr. Opal.

"Una?" I said.

"Mmmm?"

"I still can't wiggle my ears."

"S'only been a week." She grinned her gappy grin. "You're gonna have to keep practicing for longer than that."

Only a week?

Really?

Only a week, and everything had changed. Just like Elsie said it would.

I was in the middle again, squished between my two favorite wanderers in the whole wide world. But this time it was me holding the reins, and behind us were seventeen more ponies, seventeen more carts. Carrying moms and dads and brothers and sisters and aunts and uncles and cousins—all looking for their eldests.

All following me.

They sang as they went.

The new song that the Rickard sisters wrote.

*"Out of my window, looking through the night*
*I can see a middler heart burn bright.*
*All across the east fields, all across the west*
*I will sing her name from wake till rest."*

They sang it sweet and loud and strong and true.

I listened close.

There were sounds under the voices.

Mr. Gebby. *Clank, clank, clunk.*

The cows calling, up at Leap Cross.

The wind rustling the leaves.

A single chirping cricket who didn't know summer was gone yet.

And there—soft as you like—the old, dead relatives, joining in.

*"Maggie, will you let us follow you?*
*Will you help us save our eldests too?*
*Maggie, will you lead us from the town?*
*Will you help us break our boundaries down?"*

A red admiral quivered down onto Melissa's back. Wide black wings and bright red stripes. Impossible to believe it used to be a caterpillar. Melissa swished it away with her tail and it fluttered off toward the boundary ahead of us.

# Epilogue

*Ker-ackkkkkkkkkk.*

Mom struck the first blow.

Dad and Trig held the ladder steady while she swung her ax right into Andrew Solsbury's neck. His head rolled clean off and cracked into two pieces in the middle of the square. Pigeons scattered and flapped, and all the parents who'd crowded around pulled their littlests back toward them.

Her second swing took out his right arm.

"Whoa." Una spoke through a mouthful of Dad's goldie pie. "Your mom means business, doesn't she?"

"Always." November air swept round my neck. I turned up the collar of my coat.

It was all Mom's idea. Destroy the statue and replace it with a monument for everyone who'd gone to camp too long ago and weren't ever coming home. There'd be names inscribed on it and everything. She wanted to see Lil and Felix and all the others remembered forever more.

"Okay—my turn now." Mrs. Chowdhry beckoned Mom down and wobbled up the ladder herself. She could hardly lift the ax, but that wasn't going to stop her. She took a good-sized chip out of his left elbow.

"Look." I pointed over toward the laundry. "There's Mayor— I mean *Tasher*—Anderson." She was standing there with her shoulders all hunched up, a wheelbarrow in front of her and Frederick by her side. She'd got the job of clearing up after we'd knocked the statue down, and Frederick'd got the job of making sure she did it.

"Oh yeah." Una stuffed her last bit of pie into her mouth.

"Don't think I'll ever get used to calling her Tasher instead of Mayor," I said.

"Maggie! Una! Guess what!" Lindi ran over, skirt floating out behind her and Jed jogging to keep up. "Sally and Deb and all the other eldests—they're up at the cemetery, chopping down the hawthorn boundary."

Una licked the crumbs off her fingers. "Really?"

I looked at Jed.

"S'true," he said.

"Course it is!" Lindi's black eyes were all gone now, and Jed's was too. "No one's stopping them. In fact"—Lindi looked behind, then leaned in toward us—"Mr. Gebby's lent them his tools, and Mayor Wetheral's up there with them! Me and Jed are going up, too, once we've had a go at Andrew Solsbury."

"Come on, Maggie." Una wiped her hands on her sweater. "Shall we go and see? Maybe we can help."

"Hold on, just a moment." Lindi brought something out of her pocket. Two small drawstring bags made from stripy cloth.

"These are for you two. One each." She placed them in our hands.

I tugged the bag open and poked my fingers inside. Tiny things. Thin and smooth. I pulled some out.

Glinting circles. Silver, purple, gold.

Una frowned. "What are they?"

"Sequins," I said. I spread them across my palm. "They're beautiful."

"They really are." Una grinned her gappy grin. "Thank you."

"I thought maybe you could use them on your summer diary next year. Or whatever you want. I made the bags myself." Lindi slipped her hand into Jed's. "Because, well, y'know, thanks. For what you did."

Jed looked at her like she was the loveliest thing that ever existed. "Come on, Lindi." He pulled her away. "I want to get my hands on that ax before the statue's all gone."

I tipped the sequins back into the bag, taking care not to drop any. I pulled the drawstring good and tight.

"Come on, Maggie." Una lifted her elbow out to the side. "Let's go up to the hawthorn."

I linked my arm through hers and we headed off toward Frog Alley.

Just like friends.

# Acknowledgments

I'd like to send my most enormous thanks to the following
people:

My editors, Brian Geffen and Kirsty Stansfield, and the fantastic teams at Henry Holt and Nosy Crow—for all their hard
work on this book.

Illustrator Matt Griffin and designer Katie Klimowicz—for
making *The Middler* utterly beautiful.

Nancy Miles—for being my agent extraordinaire and cham-
pioning *The Middler* all the way.

The teachers and students from Bath Spa University's
MAWYP, especially the very talented class of 2016—for their
friendship, wisdom, and honesty.

My first creative writing teacher, Nicky Morris, and all my
brilliant fellow *What-nots*—for believing in my writing from
the very start.

Jodie Hodges and Jenny Savill—for encouragement and
ideas along the way.

Margaret—for endless support.

Simon, Dennis, and Victor—for simply being the most excellent people I know.

Janice, Alan, and Claire—for being my mum, dad, and sister. Without them, Maggie wouldn't be Maggie, because I wouldn't be me.